HATE IS SUCH A STRONG WORD

HATE IS SUCH A STRONG WORD

SARAH AYOUB

HarperCollins*Publishers*

HarperCollins*Publishers*

First published in Australia in 2013
by HarperCollins*Publishers* Australia Pty Limited
ABN 36 009 913 517
harpercollins.com.au

HarperCollins*Publishers*
Level 13, 201 Elizabeth Street, Sydney NSW 2000, Australia
Unit D, 63 Apollo Drive, Rosedale, Auckland 0632, New Zealand
A 53, Sector 57, Noida, UP, India
1 London Bridge Street, London SE1 9GF, United Kingdom
2 Bloor Street East, 20th floor, Toronto, Ontario M4W 1A8, Canada
195 Broadway, New York NY 10007, USA

National Library of Australia Cataloguing-in-Publication data:

Ayoub, Sarah, author.
   Hate is such a strong word / Sarah Ayoub.
   978 0 7322 9684 1 (paperback)
   978 1 7430 9916 2 (ebook)
   For ages 12+
   Families – Juvenile fiction. Interpersonal relations in adolescence –
   Juvenile fiction.
   Violence – Juvenile fiction. Lebanese Juvenile fiction.
A823.4

Cover design by Hazel Lam, HarperCollins Design Studio
Cover images by shutterstock.com
Author photograph by Simona Janek, GM Photographics
Typeset in Bembo Std by Kirby Jones
Printed and bound in Australia by McPherson's Printing Group
The papers used by HarperCollins in the manufacture of this
book are a natural, recyclable product made from wood grown in
sustainable plantation forests. The fibre source and manufacturing
processes meet recognised international environmental standards,
and carry certification.

To my parents, Tony and Yolla Ayoub, who gave my wonderful life its strong foundations, necessary guidance, and constant love

1

I hate spending New Year's Eve alone

Breathe, I tell myself. A sense of dread settles over me. There are only two possible outcomes of what I'm about to do, and honestly, will either of them impact my life that much? I pause to think it over. Yes! I need a positive outcome. I can't stomach the idea of things remaining the same. The same and I are sworn enemies. The thought of another year of sameness is about as inviting as sticking needles in my eyes.

Oh God, I'm ranting. I hope to heaven I don't rant when I make my speech. I decide against a final practice run in front of the mirror and make my way to my bedroom door.

A whiney voice stops me the moment I get outside. 'Sophie, Viola says that one day I'll grow hair in weird places all over my body and Mum'll take it off with a sticky sugar sauce she keeps in the freezer and that it really hurts.'

I look into the pleading eyes of my five-year-old sister. Surely I should shield her from the realities of pubic hair while I can? After all, at seventeen, I'm barely prepared to accept them as part of my life.

'Marie, honey, can we talk in five minutes maybe? I'm about to do something really important.'

'But, Sophie, she says it burns!'

The deep breathing is no longer working. Panic is setting in. I'm forgetting what I want to say. I sink to the floor so I'm face to face with my favourite little person, and brush her fringe away from her face.

'Baby, it's nothing you need to worry about, I swear to you. Did you run away from Angela?' I'd asked Angela, my thirteen-year-old sister, to keep the little ones distracted while I psyched myself up for my speech. 'I just really need some time alone to talk to Daddy because there's a party at Dora's house, and I was meant to be there, like, five minutes ago.'

The door swings open and my father looms in the doorway.

'Daddy! Sophie wants to go to a party at Dora's tonight,' Marie pipes up. 'If she gets to watch the fireworks, then I want to stay up too!'

I listen in despair. This isn't how it was supposed to happen.

'Is that so?' Dad says, ruffling Marie's hair but looking at me.

I nod pleadingly, cursing the fact that all the logical arguments I'd prepared for going out tonight have come down to one nod.

'Sophie knows that we're going out tonight and we need someone to babysit,' Dad tells Marie. 'And there's no one more responsible to look after our little baby than our biggest baby.'

Marie squeals in delight as he tickles her, then runs out of the room.

I find my voice. 'Dad, please. This is the first time I've ever asked to go to a New Year's party. Dora's parents and her entire family will be there so there's nothing for you to worry about.'

'That may be the case, Sophie, but I can't leave the girls home alone. Break and enters are at their worst on nights like this. What if someone comes in while the girls are watching TV? They wouldn't even hear them.'

'What about Andrew?' I ask, desperate. 'He's old enough, and it's not like they're really babies. He just has to be here, doesn't he?'

Dad looks at me like I've just suggested the big bad wolf should babysit his daughters. 'Oh, Sophie, boys don't babysit, you know that. Now give Dora a call and apologise to her from me personally. It's no big deal, I'm sure you girls can catch up tomorrow.'

I close my eyes in frustration at the blatant sexism. When I open them Mum is emerging from the ensuite brandishing a curling iron.

'What's going on?' she asks cheerfully.

I look from her to Dad and roll my eyes. 'I'm finishing off another scintillating year at home, babysitting. Because apparently I skipped adolescence altogether and am now a mother of four.'

—⁓—

I take my phone out onto the veranda, where I can watch the sun set over Bankstown, the area I've lived in since I was born. Although it's still daylight, boys are setting off illegal fireworks despite their mothers' fearful warnings. Older girls are heading out to parties, all dressed up, while their fathers lament their daughters' short childhoods and even shorter skirts. And I lament the fact that I won't be attending the globe's biggest party tonight – even in the limited way I've come to expect as a social nobody.

I can't decide which is worse: being sick of always missing out, or constantly having to explain why I'm missing out, which, trust me, is just as humiliating.

I call my best friend, Dora Maloor, to deliver the verdict.

'Nawwwww,' she wails. 'Why does he always limit your socialising to people who share your DNA?'

'I dunno,' I mumble, trying to keep myself from crying. I'm ashamed to admit that I care so much, even to her. 'Have fun on my behalf.'

'I'm sick of having fun on your behalf, Skaz,' she says. 'You've got an unhealthy attitude for a seventeen-year-old. You need to build up the courage to express yourself. It's the only way you're going to have the fulfilling life experience you subconsciously desire.'

I roll my eyes. 'What new-age hoo-ha have you been reading? That doesn't even make any sense.'

'Well, neither does a seventeen-year-old who can't stand up to her father.'

'Seriously, what am I supposed to do?'

'Um, stand up for your right to enjoy your youth,' she says, stating the obvious. 'His Stone Age 1950s Lebanese village rules have got to go. What's the reason this time? He's usually okay with you coming over.'

'One of their friends is holding a dinner at his restaurant tonight. Mum doesn't really want to go, but she is, so I have to babysit.'

'A dinner beats the little backyard soirée that my brother and sister are throwing. Although at least at my house there'll be hot boys to perve at, even if my brother's friends smile patronisingly at me.'

'At least someone's smiling at you,' I point out.

We chat for a bit longer, then I hang up and lie sprawled on the veranda floor, resisting the urge to strangle myself with the cord of my pink mobile extension handset, something Mum bought me after seeing a daytime TV segment on the effects of mobile phone radiation on the brain.

I know no one will hassle me out here, but I also find it ironic that my safe haven represents everything that bothers me. Hiding on the veranda allows me to see the outside world, but there's no way I can touch it. It just stretches out before me, while the ties of my upbringing keep my feet firmly rooted in my father's house.

I turn to look through the glass sliding doors at what's holding me back. Mum is eyeing herself in her bedroom mirror as she applies a particularly unflattering shade of red lipstick. I hear her complaining about her wrinkles, and how a new year is only going to age her. Dad is watching the LBC news direct from Lebanon, totally unaware that Mum's ramblings are his cue to say something loving or supportive.

She focuses her attention on me instead, muttering something to herself before yelling, 'Sophie, stop wiping the floor with your clothes and come here and help me.'

I scramble inside.

'God give me patience,' she wails in Arabic, raising both hands in the air. 'God give me patience to endure the torment of watching my practically adult daughter lying on the floor and catching dust that I'll have to handwash out of her clothes.'

'Mum, your floor's cleaner than the plates of most restaurants because of your incessant need to clean it!'

She gives me a look and I decide to drop the attitude. I don't want her giving me a job to do when I just want to whinge. I stand there for what seems like ages while she fiddles with her hair, her shirt, her jewellery.

'Sophie, do I look fat?' she asks eventually.

I wince, hoping she doesn't see. 'No, Mama. You look lovely.'

My white lie doesn't convince her. She looks in the mirror, eyeing the body her children have given her.

A career woman might pass my mum in the street, see her wide hips, lined face and tired movements, and pity her because of the choices she's clearly made in life – to live for others. But Mum doesn't see it that way.

'A housewife is a career woman, Sophie,' she often tells me. 'She work every day, but she doesn't make money, she makes people. She turns a lazy man into a hard-working husband, and together they grow smart, strong babies like you. Well, until the baby is seventeen and tells me she's not hungry and won't eat the *shish barak* I make for her.'

I used to love my mother's *shish barak*. The little dumplings of mincemeat smothered in warm yoghurt sauce were just the cure after a tough day in primary school when I'd worn the wrong uniform and she'd have to come and save me from detention. Nowadays, she knows I won't let her save me. Hell, I don't even tell her what's wrong any more.

But where do I start with what's wrong? Not going anywhere on New Year's is the tip of the iceberg. I feel like I don't have a say in my own life. It's as though I'm invisible, defined only in the relative: dependable daughter, sister, student and friend. Is it so wrong that I want a little more?

—◆◆◆—

'Sophieeeeee!' Marie's screeching echoes through the house the moment my parents leave.

I find her standing with folded arms outside the study. 'Angela won't let me in. She's watching something that's M-rated!' She stamps her foot and gives me a look that implies she's a victim of great injustice.

I calm her down and open the study door. 'Seriously, Ang, you're going to let the kid scream the house down? And I'm not even going to point out that *Pretty Little Liars* isn't appropriate viewing for a thirteen-year-old.'

'Sophie, we can't keep letting her have her way because she's little,' Angela says.

'No, but we can let her have her way tonight because my sanity can't take any more. Please, Ang, I'm a seventeen-year-old loser. Let me be at peace with my misery.'

She rolls her eyes. 'Okay, but I don't want to be your therapist. You're making me scared of growing up. Go let it all out in a journal or something.'

I don't budge and she sees my desperation.

'I'll go watch TV in Mum and Dad's bedroom,' she says finally, relenting. 'But I'm taking some chips with me so you'll have to bail me out if Mum finds out I've been eating upstairs.'

I give her a hug in thanks and go up to my room to avoid any more screaming matches. I figure I might as well let them sort it out themselves since they aren't going to listen to me anyway.

I change into my pyjamas, sit on my bed and open my laptop. Then I realise I don't want to go onto Facebook out of fear of what I'll see there: pictures of my classmates having fun at the kinds of parties I'm not allowed to attend. Perhaps Angela's suggestion to start a journal is a good idea, after all.

After shuffling around in my drawers, I pull out a beautiful powder-blue notebook that my Aunty Leila gave me for Christmas. Maybe this could be my sounding board. A place where I can rant about having the world's strictest dad and living by a cultural code that's at odds with my time and place. Where I can express myself without the fear of being accused of shaming my community, my family and the traditions of a heritage I'm not sure I fully grasp. A place where I can divulge my innermost thoughts, agony by agony, worry by worry, hate by hate.

Hours pass until the midnight sky is suddenly illuminated by bursts of colour, and I hear boys in the street yelling and laughing. In houses all around me, people are sharing hugs, kisses and good wishes, while I'm alone with my journal. As the firecrackers subside and a quiet darkness returns, I sit upright in my bed and write the opening words of my first entry:

I hate spending New Year's Eve alone.

2

I hate that the actions of a minority can influence the opinions of the majority

I call Dora the next day to wish her Happy New Year and find out how the party went.

'The Sophie-watch vigilance has gone up ten thousand notches,' I tell her, 'and for once, my dad's ideas on how good Lebanese girls should behave has nothing to do with it.'

'Huh?' she says, yawning loudly. 'What are you talking about? And why do you always have so much energy in the morning?'

'Dude, it's twelve fifteen. No longer morning. I assume that you haven't read the news then?'

'Skaz, when do I ever read the news?'

'Okay, checked Facebook?'

'Nope, your call literally woke me up.'

'See, this is why you never get your assignments done,' I say. 'You sleep for half the day whenever you don't have school. You even sleep *in* school if it's a boring lesson. But

I'm getting sidetracked. There's been a race riot. Well, sort of. A fight, I think. Last night. It was bad.'

'Where, how, what happened?' she asks, suddenly sounding wide awake.

'I'm not sure. From what I've read, there was some party at a house in Brighton and a few Aussie guys were out the front drinking when a group of young Lebanese guys walked past on their way to the beach. One of the Aussies made some racist joke, and the Leb boys decided it would be a good opportunity to start a punch-up.'

'No way, just there on the street? That's dramatic.'

'Trust me, it gets better,' I say sarcastically. 'The Leb guys called their friends and then the whole thing escalated until, like, half the street was involved. It was chaos until the cops came to break it up.'

'And did they?'

'Well, it took a lot of them, but yeah, they sorted it out,' I say. 'And you'll never believe who was there. Zayden's cousin in Year Ten. He got injured.'

'No freaking way! That little shit from Year Ten was in a big brawl that made it onto the news? Are you kidding me?'

'He wasn't there at the start,' I tell her. 'But apparently word got around fast and he managed to get there in time to join in. And, of course, my parents saw him - out of all the people they don't know - on the news, bruised and bleeding and flanked by two cops.'

'Whoa, that's bad,' she says. 'You reckon it'll get worse?'

'It did, this morning! People in that street woke up to find their bins turned over, their car windows smashed, fences vandalised, mailboxes broken and God knows what else. Some of it was captured on CCTV. It looks really bad.'

Dora sighs. 'It sounds bad. I mean, I get the first part – our guys ought to defend themselves if people are insulting them. But I don't get why they had to go back for more. Like, why go back and make it worse?'

'Beats me,' I say. 'I can't believe we actually know someone who was involved. I wonder if George is okay. Andrew's still in his room so I haven't had a chance to ask him.'

The doorbell rings and Mum calls out my name.

'Aaaannd that's my signal to go,' I tell Dora. 'We've got a big family lunch here today, with all my little cousins and aunties and uncles. I'd be hiding in my room if Leila wasn't coming. Talk to you later, I guess.'

'Ciao, bella,' she says, hanging up.

—⁂—

After we've eaten our body weight in food, we sit in the backyard to have dessert. I'm next to my Aunty Leila, Dad's only sister (and the thorn in his side) and the closest thing I have to an older sister.

Dad has a love/hate relationship with Leila, mainly because she's the kind of person who never listens to anyone else's opinion. She's always reminding Dad that she isn't his problem and he should leave her alone, but because their parents are dead he thinks it's his duty to make sure she behaves according to his standards.

Part of me thinks Leila's so different because she's the youngest by a long shot and was spoilt rotten by their parents. She's also the only one of their kids who was born and raised here, before the Lebanese community got so big they started taking over entire suburbs and using each other to reinforce their traditions.

I know Dad wants Leila to be married with children, but she's never done the conventional Lebanese thing. I mean, there was the time she got engaged to an Asian guy a few days after her nineteenth birthday; the time she went on some sabbatical to Bali and refused to answer any of Dad's calls; and the time she got a massive tattoo of a unicorn across her back. According to Dad, these kinds of things 'damage' her reputation and automatically give him the right to interfere and 'take care of her'.

Uncle Anthony brings up the Brighton brawl, as the media are calling it, and Leila rolls her eyes.

'Is something wrong, sister?' he asks.

'It's going to be like the Cronulla riots all over again,' she says. 'For weeks the media's going to sensationalise it, and every day they'll get someone new to talk about it – questioning whether Australia's racist, whether Lebanese people belong here, confusing the public about who Lebanese people actually are. When all it really comes down to is some drunk guy telling a lame joke and some stupid boys who like to solve problems with their fists. It's ridiculous.'

'What's ridiculous is what happened after,' Dad says. 'Even Marie has more sense than to retaliate like a child in the dead of the night. Such shame on our people! At least before we could say it was a silly disagreement in the street. Now it looks like our community has done worse than the Aussies because they took it too far.'

'What I want to know is who these people are,' Aunty Paula says, waving her hands in front of her. 'I can't imagine a grown man vandalising cars. Grown men march in the street, they hold protests, they organise peaceful demonstrations, they talk to the police. This is either the work of silly children who think themselves adults, or people who genuinely do not belong in this country. Our community needs to alienate them for its own benefit.'

'All I can say is I'm so glad I can trust my children,' Dad says, smiling at me.

'Hear, hear,' Leila replies, squeezing my arm.

Mum looks worried. 'I hope there is not a riot protesting against Lebanese people again. We've all worked very hard to make a good contribution to this country.'

'Which is why we need to make sure our children are extra safe and extra careful wherever they go,' Dad says. 'So sad that this is going to give people even more ammunition to think of us as outsiders.'

Everyone nods in agreement, even Andrew, no doubt burdened by the fact that one of his friends could have gotten seriously hurt over something so silly.

—∿—

The rest of the school holidays pass by with little fanfare. We'd started our HSC work in the last term of Year Eleven, so I spend most of the break doing assignments or turning my class notes into study notes and mind maps. Even I have to laugh at my OCD organisational skills, but considering just about no one except Dora calls to hang out with me, there isn't much else to do.

The rest of the time I read books I've borrowed from the local library – *Juliet* by Anne Fortier, *The Girl in Times Square* by Paullina Simons and *Revolution* by Jennifer Donnelly – or sit on the veranda instagramming pictures of my DIY nail art and wishing there was somewhere to go that wouldn't involve strategic planning or my parents accompanying me.

The fact that I hardly hear from anyone unless they have a homework question makes me worry even more about my invisibility complex. It's not like I don't have friends. I talk to the majority of people at school – it's just that sometimes I feel like we're all living in a big bubble. I've been at the same Catholic Lebanese school since kindergarten, and most of the time I like the fact that we have the same heritage. Our parents have all fled war; they've all started again from scratch, working hard to give their kids a better life, sending them to a school that will uphold the old traditions. But even with that in common, I *still* feel so different to them. Like I can't really understand them, and they can't understand me. Which isn't exactly an ideal basis for profound friendships.

One day, after I've taken Angela, Viola and Marie to the movies, Dora calls and asks if I want to meet her at the shops so we can grab a pie from the bakery and have a mini-picnic in the park.

'I'm in the middle of folding clothes,' I say. 'Give me about fifteen minutes and I'll ask Mum.'

As I hang up the phone Mum walks into the room.

'Aww, you're folding the clothes for me?' she says. 'Thanks so much, sweetie. You've just given me the night off to enjoy my Egyptian soap.'

'You're welcome. But, Mum, I need to ask you something.'

'Ah, is this what the Australian people call a catch?'

'No catch, I promise. I was already folding when Dora called. She wants to know if I can go meet her at the shops. We're going to get a few things and have a picnic.'

'Sophie, there's still *mjadra* from last night's dinner. Who is going to eat it if you go out?'

'Um, your other children and your husband,' I point out. 'Come on, Mum, please! It's not my fault you always cook enough to feed a small village. If you made a little less we wouldn't have leftovers.'

Mum raises her hands to the sky. 'Why do you let her question me? She is fourteen years old and barely hatched out of her egg, just a little chick, and she already wants to go around making her own plans,' she wails in Arabic.

I roll my eyes. 'I'm seventeen, remember? And I just want to eat a pie with Dora. It's not like I'm taking a gap year in Morocco to become the muse of a South American vegan artist who believes in free love.'

She stares at me blankly.

'Please?' I beg. 'I took the girls to watch that stupid kids' movie today. Let me do something for me.'

'Mmm-hmm,' she says absent-mindedly, inspecting my folding. She makes a face at me.

'What?' I ask, confused.

'Sophie, you're practically twenty years old and you can't even fold the towels properly. What's going to happen when you have your own home to look after?'

I shake my head. 'Three minutes ago I was fourteen and a chick. Now, because I can't fold towels to your liking, I'm old enough to be a woman with her own home?'

She sighs, then nods towards the door. 'Fine, go. But I expect you back in two hours.'

I kiss her on the cheek and hurry to my room to grab my wallet.

'And don't talk to anyone we don't know,' she calls after me. 'I don't need your father breathing down my neck because you're going out so much.'

I walk the five blocks to our local shopping strip. As I weave through the crowds and pass the different ethnic shops, I wonder if our lifestyle contributed to the Brighton Brawl. To outsiders, parts of Bankstown can be very confronting. Sometimes even I feel like they're not in Australia. The banks and meat-pie shops and supermarkets that used to be on this strip are all gone. There's just one fish and chip shop left, and one hot bread shop, and they're both run by Asians. Except for the newsagency and video rental store, all the rest are Lebanese shops. Hairdressing and beauty salons run by women straight out of beauty school and straight into marriage and mortgages; bakeries that sell Lebanese bread and pizza; a giant mixed grocer that imports goods direct from the Middle East; and Lebanese butchers that guarantee their meat as *halal* and know what you need to make *kibbe*.

I'm not saying there's anything wrong with this. I love that I can eat pork rolls, *shawerma* or fish and chips anytime I want, and that there's so much culture in my suburb. But I can't help wondering if in the process of trying *not* to forget where we came from, we've forgotten the country we've come to.

I stop philosophising as soon as I spot Dora, thankful for a break in my thoughts. We go inside the bakery and she buys a meat pie and vanilla slice, while I choose a potato pie and mini fruit flan.

'So much bad stuff,' I say, grinning.

She makes a face. 'Here's hoping we'll still fit into our uniforms.'

We're about to head to the park when we see two mothers whose daughters are in the grade below ours. One of them calls out my surname. Dora rolls her eyes, but I stop to talk to the woman. I have no choice. She knows my family, and the last thing I need is some gossipy mother telling everyone that Theresa Kazzi's daughter was rude.

'Hello, Mrs Chahine,' I say, my eyes pleading for Dora to come and join me.

Dora ignores me and takes a mouthful of her pie.

'Can you believe what happened in Brighton the other week?' Mrs Chahine says.

'I know, how bad was it?' I reply, shaking my head. 'Such a shame. I hope it doesn't reflect too badly on the community.'

'Indeed,' she says, looking like she couldn't care less. 'I heard that some of the boys from your school were involved. Is that true?'

Suddenly her desire to talk to me makes sense: she wants information. I'm tempted to tell her it's none of her business, but she'd only label me disrespectful and my mother a bad parent.

'A boy in Year Ten was hurt,' I admit.

Mrs Chahine's friend's eyes light up. 'Which one?'

'Um, George Saab,' I say uncomfortably.

She looks at Mrs Chahine. 'Who?'

'You'd know his parents,' Mrs Chahine replies. 'His father is the painter, and his mother is from that village near Zgharta. She drives a red Mitsubishi SUV.'

The woman nods. 'Ah yeah, I know the ones.' Her eyes widen. 'Wow, so their son was there?'

'Um, yeah,' I say, my face reddening.

'Anyone else that you know of?' they ask, oblivious to my discomfort.

'Don't you even want to ask if he's okay?' Dora says behind me. She gives them a look and grabs my hand. 'Let's go, Sophie.'

The women stare at her disdainfully, but I'm glad my telepathic begging to be rescued has finally gotten through to her.

Lebanese gossip is the bane of my existence. Lebanese women know everything; they're magnets for information on all things from real estate (they're constantly trying to recruit relatives from Lebanon to the area) to the latest marriages and divorces, family dramas and church events.

'Thanks so much for saving me,' I say as we walk to the park. 'Although it took you a while. You like seeing me miserable, don't you?'

'It's your fault. Why didn't you just fob them off?'

'I can't. They knew who I was. It'd get back to my parents.'

Dora gives me a pointed look. 'For someone who supposedly sees through all the cultural bull, you care way too much.'

'Let me remind you of Elias Kazzi's manifesto,' I say, and put on a deep voice. 'There are some things that are simply unacceptable among our people, Sophie. You must remember that. And a mistake on the part of an individual will always have consequences for others.' I go back to my normal voice. 'Seriously, what do you expect from me?'

'You act like there's a mini version of him sitting on your shoulder,' Dora says. 'Live a little.'

'It's easy for you – your parents both grew up here. Mine are still wrapped up in the old country, just like plenty of others. If I do something bad, there are other parents like them who won't let their sons date my sisters because I was rebellious.'

'I don't get that bullshit,' Dora says. 'I'm so glad my parents don't buy into it either. You know my cousin Elaine's in-laws didn't think she was suitable for their son because her parents were divorced?'

'My point exactly. Like, how the hell is that her fault? Divorce isn't contagious or hereditary. Maybe my dad is the way he is because he's trying to protect us from people like that. Half these stories happened a decade ago. People are still talking about how the Alachi family's son gambled away his house to fund his crystal meth habit.'

'Crazy stuff. I reckon that people will talk whether or not we do the right thing, so we might as well do what we want.'

Easier said than done, I think as we arrive at the park.

3

I hate that I can't keep up with the rules of high school

Over the next few days, I notice that Andrew's bedroom door is often closed. It's disconcerting – normally he leaves it wide open and the whole house reverberates with the sound of his violent action movies and video games.

I knock, hoping he has time for a quick chat. Ignoring his angry 'What?', I go in. Andrew's lying on the bed, staring at the ceiling and doing a whole lot of nothing.

'Hey,' I say, smiling. 'Can you answer a few questions for me? It's for an assignment I'm doing for Society and Culture.'

He rolls his eyes, then gestures for me to take a seat on the bed. 'What's the assignment?'

'It's a methodology – a big essay and analysis thingy – on asylum seekers. I want to look at what happens once they leave the detention centres, how well they integrate into the community, what they're doing for work, whether they participate in wider society, and whether any of that affects their cultural identity.'

'You actually chose to do that?' he says, wide-eyed.

I nod. 'Yep. I'm the only one in the class doing it so I'm hoping to do well. I've volunteered to go to a detention centre with one of the nuns from school every Thursday afternoon during Lent, so I can give the assignment a personal angle. I guess I'm trying to prove that you can retain your cultural identity and still integrate into the community without it causing social problems. It's going to be a lot of work.'

'But what's the point?' he asks, sitting up. 'Maybe it's the wider Aussie community that needs to adjust to the idea of migration. If they didn't have a problem with other cultures, there wouldn't be any riots.'

'Yeah, but we don't know what leads to events like that. Maybe people feel like they're losing their identity because other cultures come in and change things – like using their own languages on shopfronts and stuff ...' He tries to interrupt, but I speak over him. 'I'm not saying that they're right – I've experienced racism too – but maybe those Leb guys at Brighton did something to incite the comment. And even if they didn't, they probably made it worse by calling others in on the fight.'

Andrew's eyes narrow, but he still answers my questions. I type up his responses afterwards and go online to do some more reading. I want to understand what sorts of things these people might be fleeing from. I'm pretty sure it'll be a mixed bag: some will be genuine refugees, while others will have chosen Australia because we have a good welfare program. I see the attraction: we're lucky to have a government that supports parents, students, the elderly and the sick, whereas in other countries some political groups shoot at girls to scare them off going to school. That makes me sick to my stomach, and I find myself signing up for updates from an organisation that's trying to help the girls in those countries get access to education.

A Facebook notification comes through while I'm reading: Vanessa's invite to her annual back-to-school party. She's been doing it every year since we started Year Nine, except this time she's evidently decided to mix up the location.

> Vanessa Saade's Back-to-School-Beach-BBQ-Bash
>
> Let's get the beach back at our Back-to-School Party!
>
> Where: Brighton Beach
>
> When: 3 February
>
> Time: 7pm
>
> Bring: Whoever you want so long as they can par-tay!
>
> RSVP: Don't bother! I mean, with me there, who cares if you make it or not? Ha ha!
>
> It's going to be the party of the year. Don't miss out!
>
> Love, hugs and kisses, Vanessa

I've barely had time to digest the invite when Dora pipes up in Facebook chat:

> Did u get the invite? I can't believe she's doing
> it at the beach this year! She'll be the first one
> calling the cops and blubbering like a baby at
> the first sign of trouble. Oh, well, at least it'll
> be something different. I could do with a little
> bit of excitement in my life right now.

I type in my reply:

> Yeah, but do you want the excitement to wind up
> on the news? I don't want to get swept up in some
> kind of dumb dipshit teenage gang payback. The
> beach is a public place, other people will turn up
> and it'll escalate. And when it does, it'll just be
> more ammo to prove our shit reputation in this
> country. Like we need it after the gang rapes and
> terror trials and whatever else.
>
> **Dora**
> You're being a drama queen again. I'm sure it
> won't be that bad.
>
> **Sophie**
> Operative word being 'that'. By the way, what's
> with what she called it? Talk about appealing
> use of alliteration lol. I think this might
> actually be the first time I don't WANT to go to
> anything!

Dora
Even if Zayden's there? ;)

Sophie
Why, because he'll notice if I'm there? He hasn't noticed me for the past five years.

Dora
Okay, so he doesn't talk to you. But he's the most popular guy in school – he doesn't have time to. He's got a horde of crazy nutbag women around him all the time so why would he notice the girl who hides behind her invisibility and avoids him?

Zayden Malouf is hot. If we were in an American teen movie, he'd be the jock with the awesome car and masses of teenage girls after him, and I'd be the nerd girl in band camp he never takes any notice of. But then something magical would happen and he'd suddenly become aware of my existence and ask me to the prom (okay, the formal) and I'd take his breath away thanks to some contact lenses, copious hours of hair straightening, fake tan and a stunning red dress. And I'd actually be allowed to go with him, of course, because my American teen-movie dad would be awesome and cool and take photos of him giving me a corsage before we left the house.

I've had a crush on Zayden since Year Eight, when he nudged me in history and asked to borrow a pencil, then admitted that he was struggling with our writing task: a diary entry from the perspective of a bushranger. I couldn't resist his call for help back then, and these days I'm even worse around him. That said, I doubt he ever thinks about me, not when there are girls like Vanessa Saade around, being flirtatious and fun and gorgeous – three things I'm certainly not.

Vanessa Saade is super confident, super sassy and super gorgeous: the cheerleading captain in the American teen movie. She's the youngest daughter of one of the local councillors, and even though her family packed up and moved to the waterfront suburb of Cabarita last year, she stayed on at our school because she's Queen Bee. She likes to lord it over a group of girls who think they're seventeen going on thirty-one – including my ex-best friend Rita Malkoun.

Rita and I used to be inseparable, but then in Year Seven she pashed a guy I liked at our swimming carnival and told me about it just to suss out my reaction. I remember being so hurt. I've never understood why she did it because she used to say she hated his guts. I tried calling her during the school holidays, but when we came back in Year Eight she pretended she didn't know me. I've been able to see right through her ever since, and what I've seen isn't pretty.

I start typing again:

> I can't help that I'm shy. And that I don't believe in girls chasing boys! I like to be romanced.

> **Dora**
> Sometimes I think you're living in your dad's Stone Age as well, you know? Whatever. Back to the agenda, because my sister's nagging for the iPad. Clearly the computer upstairs is too far

away for her lazy ass. So, are we gonna go to
the 'par-tay'?

Sophie
Yeah, right. My dad has to call something
akin to a UN Conference to decide if I can go
Thursday-night shopping at Westfield. There's
no way in hell he's letting me go to a party
at Brighton, or any beach right now. He's still
worried about Cronulla all those years ago! In
fact, he's milking the 'racism' for all it's worth
and using it as his own personal justification
for keeping me home. And loving it, no doubt.

Dora
You need to stop being a wuss and just ask
your dad! Talk to him, Sophie! You're going into
Year Twelve, for God's sake. There's gonna be
a whole lot more of this crappy social stuff. My
sister says it's all part of the experience of high
school and we don't wanna miss out. I know I
don't want to, I want this year to be different for
me too. So PLEEEAASSSE try! At least so your
dork of a friend isn't there on her lonesome. And
call me as soon as you've asked him. Geez, gtg,
Jade's killing me to get on the iPad. I wonder if
we're going to be old and love online shopping
more than Facebook chat one day? Toodles xx

I laugh out loud. Miss the experiences of high school? I've
been doing that for the past five years; I've become a pro at it.

I walk the school corridors more invisible than the cleaner, blending so far into the background that it feels like I belong there.

—◊—

I go downstairs to ask Dad permission, wondering if this time is going to be any different. I have to be strategic. On the one hand, I've been the epitome of teenage daughter perfection the past few weeks, pouting only a little when I feel I've suffered yet another injustice, and helping out around the house and with my sisters as much as possible. On the other, as the eldest child, and a female at that, I'm used to a level of security similar to that of presidents and royals. I've spent most of my adolescence accepting the fact that I'm not allowed to go to parties or school get-togethers. But Dora's right, this year is different. I'm almost eighteen, and in a matter of months I'll be done with school and moving into the real world, and there's nothing Dad can do to stop it.

I start psyching myself up, bummed that this time I can't use Andrew as leverage. At fifteen, he's usually allowed to go out with no questions asked, purely because he's male and therefore less likely to be judged by our conservative Lebanese society. But lately he hasn't been going out; he's just been hanging at home staring at the ceiling.

I call out to my parents before I enter the living room. 'Mum, Dad?'

'*Eh, habibi,*' Mum says, without glancing up from her zucchini stuffing. She's sitting on the floor, a giant bowl of rice and meat in front of her, a tray piled high with zucchinis on the coffee table beside her. 'What can I do you for?' she asks.

She's just learnt that phrase from one of the older ladies down the street and loves it. Dad presses mute on the Arabic news. Good sign: he's willing to forego the dramas of Beirut and the latest stuff-up of another politician to hear me out.

'As you know,' I begin, 'I'm starting Year Twelve properly this year. My first term of the HSC last year went pretty well and I got pretty good grades. I'm very focused on what I want out of this year academically, but at school they're also encouraging us to participate in non-academic things, to strengthen our friendship as a class and to better equip us socially when we leave school.'

Dad shifts, a curious look on his face. Oh boy. Meanwhile Mum looks like she doesn't understand half the words that are coming out of my mouth. I throw in a bit of Arabic for good measure.

'Next Friday night my class is having a get-together, just a hangout really, a way of having some fun before we settle down for the term. Dora's mum can take us and bring us back, so you won't have to do anything at all. And I'll be back home at midnight, so it won't be a late night.'

'Is this held at the school, Sophie?'

'Um, no, Dad. Vanessa Saade, the school's vice-captain, is throwing it. There won't be any teachers there.'

'Ah, okay, I see. And her parents, do I know them? Which village do these Saades come from? What does her father do?'

Knowing which village in Lebanon someone's from is the equivalent of doing a police background check on them. People from certain villages who've been in Australia for ages are more liberal in their lifestyles (their daughters can go on holiday with a group of friends, even if males are present), while others are so traditional they expect their daughters to marry distant cousins over 'outsiders' from other villages.

'I'm not sure of the village, Baba. But her dad's on the local council. They live in Cabarita or something.'

'Do you know him, Elias?' Mum asks.

Dad fancies himself a bit of a socialite, and the Saades' wealth makes them fair game.

'*La*, Theresa. No, I don't know him personally, but I know of him. As long as the parents will be there, it is okay. Sophie is becoming a big girl, after all.'

Ooh, the clincher. I wait for the inevitable.

'Will they be there, Sophie?'

'I'm not sure, Dad. I can't say either way.'

'You didn't ask the girl? Ask her. It makes a big difference, this supervision.'

I shift uncomfortably. 'Dad, sorry, but I feel weird asking. We're not that close. I don't even have her mobile.'

This is a lie. Everyone has Vanessa Saade's mobile. Even me, despite my blending-into-the-background status. But I know that if I ring to ask that particular question, she'll belittle me for the rest of the school year.

'Well, then, you're not close. You don't need to go to her party. Stay at home and do something with us. You can see all your friends at school.' He unmutes the news. 'Next week you start, eh? The big Year Twelve, my little baby.'

'But, Dad, please! Everyone will be there, and I promise I'll be home at a decent hour. You know that I'm responsible and well-behaved.'

He responds without even looking at me, his eyes fixed on the screen. 'I know that, *habibi*. But it's everyone else's behaviour I worry about, not yours. Besides, those house parties are always an occasion for trouble. I don't like the way these kids dance so close together like Leanna and Nicki Mirage on the TV that Vee is always watching. Their closes are the size of your sister Marie's!'

'It's Rihanna, Dad,' I say, on the brink of tears. 'And Minaj. And clothes, not closes. But, Dad, I'm not one of those girls, and you know that.'

'Is it at her house?' asks Mum.

Ohh, so close.

'Err, no. It's at the beach.'

I don't need to tell them which one, because if the look they've just exchanged is anything to go by, they already know.

'I don't know why you bothered to ask, Sophie. That's ten times worse and it's an absolute no. No, no, no, no, no.'

I quickly spin around and head for my room, not wanting Dad to see the tears streaming down my face.

Cursing Vanessa Saade for her desire to stand out, I climb into bed wondering if things are ever going to change. At this point, it seems like my resurrection from Miss Prim and Nerdy to something a little more acceptable is never going to happen.

Dora had asked me to call her with Dad's response, but I'm too upset to chat so I write a quick email.

From: skazzi58@hotmail.com
To: dorkus_maloorkus@hotmail.com
Subject: The Answer
Surprise, surprise – he said no! It started off really well too, but as soon as he found out it was at a beach, he skitzed it. I can so tell you what he was thinking:

* Sex trap – on account of the fact that it's at some beach where there'll no doubt be dim light, boys with no shirts on and zero adult supervision.

* Recently infamous public place – plenty of hoodlums, bums and drunk racists who'll attract the attention of news crews.

* Not fit for good Lebanese girls, who belong at home with their loving and nurturing (read: oppressive) fathers. Because a girl who goes to parties at the beach will never ensnare a respectable Lebanese husband.

Oh well, that's life. I shouldn't have gotten my hopes up to begin with.

You know the drill: GO, HAVE FUN, DOCUMENT EVERYTHING, FORGET NOTHING. First thing at school on Monday, I want a dramatic play-by-play that makes me feel as though I was there.

Adios amiga xx

—⁓—

Dad comes into my room early on the morning of the party. I'm hoping he's going to tell me he's had a change of heart, but really I know for that to happen I'd have to be still asleep and dreaming.

I pretend I'm asleep, but peek at him as he hovers around my bookshelf and picks up a picture of him and me dancing at a wedding when I was nine. He holds the frame with both hands, staring at me in a frilly pink party dress and mary-janes, my hair in braids, standing on his toes.

I stir, and he turns to me and smiles. 'You are growing up too fast for my liking, baby Soph,' he says in Arabic.

'Hey, Dad,' I say flatly.

'The big party tonight, ay?'

'Dad, please don't remind me. I don't want to talk about it.' *Especially to you.*

'Sophie, you can't hide in your room every time something doesn't go your way. That is not fair. You need to negotiate with me.'

I roll my eyes, but luckily he doesn't see.

'I want to know why a party in a faraway public place, where there have been problems recently, and where there is no adult supervision, is so important to you. You said it yourself – you are a responsible girl. At least at a party at a house we can ring the parents, or know where to go if something goes wrong. Don't you understand that we worry? I don't see why they had to have it so far away, after everything that's happened this summer. It's just asking for trouble.'

I want to tell him that I would've preferred the party to be in Vanessa's backyard too so I could've left early when I inevitably realised I'm no match for the girls there. But I don't want to agree with him on anything right now, so I stay silent.

I don't tell him the real reason I'm bummed is because I'd been hoping that after seventeen years of being the perfect Lebanese daughter he'd give me a little free rein during my last year of school. A year in which I might hopefully change my status to something other than the resident Plain Jane of Cedar Saints College. A year in which I might do something to be remembered by.

I want to tell him a lot of things, but they are things he wouldn't understand because he doesn't really know me or the reality of the world I live in, and I don't really know him. All I want to do is grow up and move on with my life, while he wants to keep me glued to the couch watching *Today Tonight* with him and not offering any opinions different from his own.

'Dad,' I say finally, 'I just want to be like all my friends – I want to have fun like other people my age. It's not fair that I'm always missing out. Is that too much to ask?'

But apparently it is, because he shakes his head in frustration and walks out muttering something about how he can never win, the ingratitude of children raised in this country, and how the parties back in his village in Lebanon were all about trustworthy friendships instead of invitations to strip ourselves of virtue or get into fighting matches that will appear on the evening news.

And people wonder where I get my drama queen traits from!

I sigh and flop back on my pillows. It isn't anything that I haven't heard before. The excuses are always the same, so much so that I've come to know them by heart.

I spend pretty much the rest of the weekend lying on my bed listening to songs by The Temper Trap over and over and purposely avoiding Facebook and gossip about Vanessa's party. I even avoid calling Dora, frightened that the party will have been fantastic and I'll be unable to keep the jealousy from my voice.

Before I know it, it's the night before the first day of school and I'm wondering what the year will bring.

Please, God, I pray, help me get out of my square before it kills me. Help me see the bigger world. Help me to stand up for myself. Let me experience life on the outside for a change. Let me live. Let me love. Just let me breathe, because I'm sick of holding my breath and waiting for life to start.

But God is all knowing and He's known my predicament for a while now, and still my prayers remain unanswered.

And then I have a horrible thought. What if I'm invisible to God too?

4

I hate that I don't belong at my school, and I hate the fact that sometimes I really, really want to

The first day back at school is usually a relief for the kids in our family. We like the routine and everything that comes with it; being busy with homework and projects gives us a little bit of independence in our big, close-knit household.

My parents' concern about our safety and wellbeing extends to us walking the few blocks to school, so Mum always drives us, which makes weekday mornings chaotic as we work around Viola's desire to be super early and Andrew's extreme lateness. For as long as I can remember, we've prayed together on the drive to school ('God, keep me from harm and evil, protect me and those I love, let your light shine in my interactions with others ...'). It's sweet but ironic, because one of us usually loses our temper as soon as we're held up by someone illegally stopping to drop off their kids.

This is Marie's first year at school so I take her into the kindy area, feeling nostalgic for the innocent fun I've had in this playground. I reach the high school grounds ten minutes before the bell for assembly – perfect timing to meet Dora just inside the school gate. I sit on a bench and watch people filing through the gate, wondering if they're filled with the same anticipation I am that things might change this year.

By five to, Dora still hasn't arrived and I find myself torn between wanting to be a good friend and a punctual student. Maybe she's sick today. I hitch my bag over my shoulder and start walking through the quadrangle, then stop in my tracks when I spot Dora sitting with Rita Malkoun and Vanessa Saade. Perhaps things are changing. I shuffle my feet a little, undecided about what to do. I don't want to hang out with girls I don't like, even though I know they have the power to pull me up the school social ladder. That would make me a hypocrite.

Thankfully Dora sees me. She grabs her backpack and comes running over. We link arms and she squeals in my ear, 'Yay! Three terms to go and we're outies!'

'Tell me about it, Maloorkus. Three terms and we finally get to make headway in the real world. You as a speech therapy student, me surrounded by other bores in an accounting course I don't want to do. Exciting!'

She looks at me pointedly. 'Stop being a pessimist. At least when you're at uni you might have more freedom. You can tell your dad you have night classes and go drink cocktails in a swanky bar instead. Maybe you'll get so drunk you'll be able to figure out what you want to do instead of just going along with your dad's wishes.'

I sigh loudly, knowing she's right. As we line up for assembly, I spot her fingernails and give her an incredulous look.

'Really, Dora? Nail polish on the first day of school? You know that Magdalena's going to punish you hard – it's not like you didn't have time to take it off over the last seven weeks.'

'Puh-lease,' she says, ignoring my warning about our super-strict headmistress. 'Miss Gerges is our homeroom teacher this year. She doesn't even check nails.'

'I guess we're lucky she's always too busy trying not to get busted herself for sneaking late into school.'

We both crack up. Miss Gerges is an ex-student who wound up with a job at Cedar Saints College in her first year out of uni. It's worked in her favour career-wise, but she's still young at heart and doesn't bother too much with discipline. She knows the students see her as one of them and she doesn't want to ruin the relationship.

The school bell rings before I get a chance to ask Dora why she was hanging out with Vanessa and Co, and before I know it we're standing in line singing the national anthem, then listening to a bunch of announcements. I wander off into philosophical-musing territory, but then my eyes rest on Zayden and I shift into teenage-girl trance instead.

He's got taller over the summer holidays – not huge, but enough to show he's leaving boyhood. His hair is shorter and it suits him; he looks older, more grown-up. He pulls a mobile out of his pocket and checks it briefly before slipping it back and whispering something into Simon Abu-Hayek's ear. They grin at each other and I turn away, ashamed of my pining.

Dora nudges me, then subtly tilts her head towards the back of the boys' line. I follow her gaze and see a guy who could pass for nineteen dressed in our school's uniform but carrying a Country Road bag. Dora raises her eyebrows at me as if saying she likes what she sees. Admittedly, there is something there worth looking at. New Boy is tall and broad-shouldered with a hint of muscle definition, not too obvious. His darkish hair and fair skin, both tinted lightly by the sun, add to his physical charm, but it's the way that he carries himself that makes him attractive: he has an air of confidence that suggests he's at ease with himself. Like the world needs another one of those.

He gives me a half-smile, half-smirk, and I turn away.

'He has gorgeous eyes!' squeals Dora.

'Shhh, don't get in trouble on your first day. And how can you see anyway? He's wearing glasses.'

'I have a radar,' she replies.

Mr Trebold gives her a look and we're quiet again, joining the hundreds of other students bemoaning the end of the summer holidays.

—〰—

My first two classes – History and Maths – go by without much excitement. At recess I wait for Dora under the tree that's been our hang-out since we became friends in Year Nine.

She bounds up to me and grabs my hand. 'Okay, I have details!'

'You're a fount of information for pathetic, bored people like myself,' I say. 'Shoot.'

She waves her hand at me dismissively. 'I don't want to have to repeat it, so hang on.'

Before I can ask her what she means, I see Vanessa, Rita and a few of their friends coming towards us.

'I think you need to tell me what's going on,' I hiss. 'Why are they coming to hang out with us? Have you forgotten how bitchy they've been to us the past few years?'

'Evidently *they* have,' she says, giving me a death stare. 'Look, I ran into Rita at a wedding, we were sitting at the same table. And then at the beach party thing … Well, basically she's not so bad, so deal with it and don't embarrass me.'

I glare at her.

'I didn't mean it like that,' she says, rolling her eyes. 'Look, you said it yourself – you don't want to be a nobody in your last year, right?' She nods in their direction. 'Well, they're your ticket out.'

Vanessa, Rita and the others put their bags down and sit on the grass, complaining the whole time about insects, how difficult it is to sit gracefully and the possibility of bird poo landing on their blow-dried hair. I want to point out that if their skirts weren't so short, sitting gracefully wouldn't be an issue. It's not like my skirt is ankle-length or anything, but at least I don't have to plan around it as I go about my day.

'So tell us what you've got, Dors,' Rita says. 'Who's the cutie pie in our class and how long do we have him for?'

I choke on my apple when she says Dors, but no one seems to notice.

'Well,' Dora says, looking around, 'you're not going to believe this. Turns out the new boy isn't even Leb! Well, he's half-Leb. His name's Shehadie Goldsmith.'

When we look puzzled, she adds, 'His mum gave him her maiden name as his first name when he was born. Weird, huh?'

I actually think it's kind of cool, but don't say so.

'His mum died about a year ago, and ever since he's been a bit of a problem for his dad. He was expelled from his last school, even though he's supposedly really smart and stuff.'

'So why'd he come here?' one of the girls asks.

'Apparently his mum was from Bankstown and her parents still live here, so his dad decided to send him to live with his grandparents. And maybe learn about his mum's culture in the process, I guess. He doesn't really know anything about Lebanon or the language or anything.'

'How do you know all this?' I ask, impressed. Dora would zone out of her own life if she could.

'Sister told Daniel Abboud to look out for him. It's kind of public knowledge now. Everyone was talking about it in Senior Science this morning.'

'Wow,' Rita says, looking at Vanessa. 'Forget cutie pie's life story, what are they doing bringing an Aussie here after what happened to Zayden's cousin?'

'What, George Saab?' I ask. 'That has nothing to do with anything. It happened in Brighton. What are the odds that the new guy even knows those boys? Just because he's Aussie – sorry, *half*-Aussie – it doesn't mean he shouldn't be welcome here.'

'He's not just a half-Aussie,' Dora says, sounding scandalised. 'He's from Cronulla! A Shire boy born and bred. Can you believe it? A full-blown Anglo gets accepted into our school in our final year?'

'Maybe they're trying to build bridges,' I say. 'Get a little flexible with the intake, open our minds up a bit. Besides, he's half-Lebanese, not full-blown Anglo. He might blend in just fine.'

Vanessa laughs. 'As if. No one's going to want to build bridges, Sophie. The fight on New Year's Eve only proves that what happened in Cronulla can happen again. Those people have no respect for our culture. And judging by the reaction of Zayden and his group, the new guy might as well be a full-on Anglo.'

'She's right,' Dora says. 'He was in my class in Standard Maths 1, and Zayden and a bunch of his friends started calling out all this stuff – go back to where you came from or whatever. He went up to Zayden and was all like, "What's your problem?" and then Zayden and his friends got all over him. It got so loud that a bunch of teachers came in from other classrooms.'

'And now the whole school knows?' I ask.

She nods. 'This guy's got no chance. Apparently during the argument someone went up and wrote, "Do they have to own the whole country and our school?" on the whiteboard.'

There's a murmur of agreement among the girls, but I'm shocked by the overt racism. Then again, I've seen people yelling 'You Lebs aren't welcome here' on national TV, so it's naive to think there wouldn't be backlash from our community.

'I reckon the new guy's going to hang out in the staffroom pretty much all day today,' Dora says. 'The teachers want us to adjust to having an outsider in our classes, but things are going to be rough for a while, I guess.'

She says the word 'outsider' like it's part of a big conspiracy.

The bell rings and I stand up, dusting the grass off my uniform. I grab Dora's hand to help her up and we make our way to the building, leaving Vanessa and the others to go to their classes.

'Wow,' I say, thankful they're gone. 'A new Aussie boy in school and hanging out with Vanessa and Co at recess. Looks like things are getting a little more exciting around here.'

—∽—

On day three, New Guy sits next to me in English. I can feel myself sweating through my school shirt in the heat, but he's wearing a navy jumper with a bulldog on it, the most revolting thing I've ever seen. It's old and ugly and looks completely out of place with his uniform. I assume he's trying to fit in with the footy fanatics who follow the Canterbury Bulldogs, and I want to tell him that he's got it all wrong and that isn't the way to get people to like him. But I don't say anything in case Zayden sees me talking to him and labels me a low-life. That'd make me even less popular than I currently am.

I have to give him points though: even in the February heat and humidity, and even though he's swathed in fleece, New Boy manages to smell good. Remarkably good, in fact. I notice that the Country Road bag has been replaced by a school backpack, which he's tried to mess up so it doesn't look so damn new.

He slides a glance at me and I nod in recognition. I'm trying for nonchalance, but even I find it ironic that I'm trying so hard to look as though I'm not trying at all.

He attempts to start a conversation, but I give him one word answers and eventually he gives up. 'All the same,' he mutters, fiddling with the zippers on his school bag.

'Excuse me?' I say, incredulous, even though I haven't been exactly friendly.

'Not one for talking, huh?' he says. 'Why am I not surprised?'

If there's one thing I hate in the world, it's being lumped into a category. 'What the hell's that supposed to mean?'

'You come to a school where the Catholic faith is supposedly so important, and you can't get a single person to acknowledge your existence. What a joke.' He shakes his head.

'Dude, what the hell is your problem? You just got here. Don't start causing trouble, because you'll get nowhere.'

Although I sound confident, inside I'm freaking out. I'm not the type to clash with people.

'*Dude*, my mere presence here is obviously a problem. All you need to do is say, "Hey, how are you? How are things going? Settling in okay?" Even if it's just a facade and, like the rest of the people in this school, you don't actually give a sh—'

Mr Trebold's loud voice interrupts us. 'Mr Goldsmith, Ms Kazzi, do you think you could resume your conversation a little later so I can get on with our English class? Unless, of course, you're talking about Shakespeare?'

'Sorry, sir,' I say, red-faced as the entire class turns around to see me fraternising with the enemy.

Like my high school life could get any worse. So much for building bridges.

5

I hate feeling like I can never win

'How come we're not waiting for Andrew?' I ask Mum as she pulls away from the kerb.

'He's going to George Saab's house,' Viola answers from the back seat. 'The boy that was bashed by the Aussies.'

I twist around from the front seat to look at her. 'I don't think that's how we should be describing it, sweetie. We shouldn't put the blame on anyone before we know what happened.'

'Whatever. Sister Mary told us that racism has no place in our classroom,' she says, talking about her new fourth grade teacher. 'But that's because she's Chinese and people have been racist to her. She said she ignores it.'

Mum glances at her in the rear-view mirror. 'Well, Vee, you're lucky you don't experience racism in your school because everyone's the same. But when you're older and at university or in a job, you should remember what your teacher told you. We should treat everyone in the way we want to be treated. There's no point going to church and calling ourselves Christian if we can't do that.'

When we get home, I help Mum unpack some groceries from the car and spot Andrew's school bag in the boot.

'How did Andrew get to George's?' I ask.

Mum pulls a face. 'Don't hate me,' she begs, 'but I let him walk.'

'Aww, Mum! That's so unfair. Why can't I walk? We don't live that far away. I could use the time to myself.'

She laughs. 'I had no idea we were such a burden to your wellbeing, Sophie.'

I don't laugh with her and she sighs.

'You know how your father feels – he just wants to protect you and keep you safe. He worries a lot. So do I. The world is a dangerous place for a young woman.'

'Oh, and I suppose nothing ever happens to boys?' I argue. 'Andrew's fifteen! I'm light years ahead of him in maturity. I don't know why you think he can take care of himself and I can't.'

'Sophie, I let you walk to meet Dora at the shops the other week.'

'I'm talking about school. I've been asking to walk to school for two years now. No one else gets questioned. Why me?'

'These are the rules for now, okay?' she says in an angry tone. 'If it makes you feel better, I'll change my mind about Andrew walking too.'

'That's not what I'm asking,' I say as I storm inside.

Later, when I am sitting on my bed doing homework, Andrew walks in.

'It's polite to knock,' I tell him.

He shrugs and points a finger at me. 'Don't you ever go questioning Mum or Dad about what I do and whether or not it's okay. They're fine with me walking, so it's none of your business. You don't need to get involved.'

I sigh. 'Sorry. I'm frustrated. I'm two years older than you and they freak out if I go to the corner shop. I don't get why you get to be different.'

He looks at me like I'm stupid. 'I'm a guy. It's just how it is.'

'Yeah, well, it's bullshit. When I have kids, my son and daughter are going to be equal. None of this girls stay at home and boys go out crap. I wouldn't want my daughter thinking she's not marriage material if she has a social life.'

'Whatever. You think too much.'

'Let me guess,' I say. 'It's bad for me to have a brain, right? I should just focus on housework.'

He gives me a half-smile. 'I'm not the one who said it.'

I smile back. It feels good to be talking again.

'Hey, I need to ask you about something,' I say after a moment. I pat the end of the bed, inviting him to sit down.

'Nah, I have to have a shower,' he says. 'So *yalla*, make it fast. Did someone say something to you? You want me to bash a guy? You need money?'

'No,' I scoff. 'And you should think twice before offering to punch people out. It's no wonder the media's blaming Lebanese guys for violence.'

'Oooft, Sophie! Tell me what you want without using your Year Twelve analysis on me.'

'Geez, sorry,' I say, putting my hands up in mock self-defence. 'It's just that you've been acting a bit strange lately. Different. Like there's something on your mind all the time that makes you worried and angry. Is everything okay at school?'

'Yeah,' he drawls.

'What about George?' I ask.

'He's fine. He's getting heaps better. No more bruising – only his right eye's still a little swollen.'

'What about Anton and Eddie?' I ask. They're Andrew's other close friends at school.

'They're good too. They came with me to visit George today. He's back at school next week, but I think it's going to be weird. His cousin Zayden's really angry about the Aussie boy in your class. George is worried about it.'

'If anything, the Aussie boy should be worried,' I say. 'At least George has people who know and support him. No one talks to the new guy.'

Andrew shrugs. 'Whatever. As long as he stays away from George. And you stay away from him. Avoid any trouble.'

I shoot him a look as he walks out the door. At least I tried.

I can't concentrate on school work after that so I call Dora.

The Optus lady answers. 'The person you have called is unavailable. To notify them of your call, please hang up after the tone.'

I hang up and send a text instead.

> Hey – what r u doing? It's been a while since we had a chance 2 talk at school. Call me, I miss chatting 2 u

I lie by the phone for five minutes waiting for a reply, then go back to reading World War I sources for my History essay. At least homework is a distraction from my depressing life.

—⁓—

Dora doesn't call me back on Friday night, or all day Saturday. When I get back from church on Sunday morning, there's a missed call and a reply to my SMS on my phone.

> hey lady bird, call me. i'm home all day and need help
> with business essay

I laugh because she can't make it through an assignment without me, then grab the phone and dial her.

'Heya,' she says when she picks up. 'How's my favourite homework saviour going?'

'I'm a lot more than your homework saviour, you cow,' I say, only half-joking. 'Where have you been?'

'You'll hate me if I tell you.'

'Tell me anyway. I insist.'

'Okay, but don't laugh. I hung out with Rita Malkoun for a bit yesterday. She called me to meet up so I went along. I never knew we had that much in common, to be honest.'

'I'm sorry,' I say incredulously. 'You *what?*'

'Yeah, I know. It's so strange, ay? But she's pretty cool if you get to know her.'

'Dora, you do know who you're talking to? She used to be my best mate, remember?'

'I know, but that was ages ago! You've both grown up and changed since then.'

'Doubt it,' I mumble.

'Well, maybe she has and you haven't. Come on, Soph, get over it! We're in Year Twelve! Everyone's gonna end up being our best friends by the time we finish.'

She has a point. Well, maybe. History (okay, TV) has shown me that people sometimes find friends in the most unexpected places. Maybe this is part of our Year Twelve bonding and growing-up process.

'I guess,' I say. 'I was just a bit concerned because you haven't had much for time for us lately. Don't forget me now that you're down with the cool chicks, okay?'

'Correction. Now that *we're* down. And in slightly more fabulous news, it means that we get to go to the Easter Dance in style in whatever ultra-suave transportation Vanessa's dad is arranging for us. No more wallflowers this year, baby!' she squeals.

'All right!' I say, mustering as much enthusiasm as I can.

Despite Dora's optimism, I can't shake the thought that things are slowly changing for the worse. Sure, we've always craved the chance to remove our invisibility cloaks, but hanging with the likes of Vanessa Saade and Rita Malkoun is bound to end in disaster. On the other hand, it could bring me closer to Zayden …

I hang up the phone, feeling anxious and confused. I know I should be excited that I'll no longer be a social outcast in my final year at school, but I'm torn between a desire to fit in and a desire to be true to myself. And if I'm being true to myself, I just don't feel comfortable hanging out with girls who are so different from me. I can't trust Rita Malkoun – she's a two-faced bitch who should come with a warning.

I spend the rest of the night wondering about the price of popularity and fun; and whether, once paid, it'd be worth it. I know I'll only really find out if I put myself in the firing line. Like I don't feel fragile enough as it is.

6

I hate looking at my generation and seeing apathy and complacency

When Lent starts, Years Ten, Eleven and Twelve have to spend an entire afternoon listening to a series of motivational talks. The idea is that Lent is a time to mull over our temptations and weaknesses and to renew our Christian faith. Although we all scoff and roll our eyes, we sit and listen intently to what each of the speakers has to say, because, as Sister Magdalena tells us, they're 'enriching our increasingly plagued lives'. I want to put my hand up and ask what's so plagued about our lives, but then I remember I'm keeping an entire journal of what plagues me and bottling up the rest like a freak, so I'm not exactly one to talk.

The speakers are a priest, who talks about how we can find strength in Christ at this 'important but sometimes difficult stage' of our lives; an ambulance driver and police officer, who warn us about the dangers of drink driving, drug abuse and speeding; and a councillor from our local government.

It's during the third talk that the trouble starts. The councillor, Edward Franks, talks about career programs at the local library, study-help sessions run by former teachers and HSC examiners, and a barbecue organised with 'sister councils' so we can meet teenagers of Anglo-Australian, Aboriginal and Islander backgrounds and learn how our lives are all similar, even though our parents come from different places.

As he finishes speaking, Zayden Malouf and his buddies make scoffing noises.

'Is there something wrong?' Councillor Franks asks.

I can see the tips of his ears turning red and think how funny it is that adults are automatically scared of antsy teenagers, especially ones the newspapers label as having a reputation for trouble.

'Yeah, there is, actually,' Zayden says in a deep, almost threatening voice. 'I want to know why you're pretending to care about us, when everyone knows the police are butting into our lives trying to find out if we were involved in those stupid attacks after those dumb Aussies started that brawl in Brighton.'

The whole room falls silent. I half-expect Councillor Franks to come up to me and ask to borrow the hole I often want to crawl into.

'What's your name, son?' he asks.

'Zayden. Zayden Malouf.'

'Err, right,' Councillor Franks responds. 'Well, young man, we can't exactly not cooperate with the police on such a matter. If we're punishing those responsible for the brawls – on both sides, I might add – then it's also fair to punish those who retaliated. That's the way things work in our country. It's all about justice and fairness.'

He smiles awkwardly and we look at him blankly. It shits me, and everyone else too, I'm sure, that he's clearly dismissed Zayden's name as being too difficult to pronounce.

'Yeah, but that's not my point,' Zayden says. 'My point is that you're arranging a barbecue when everything's still fresh, like you're expecting it to solve the problem. Don't forget that more than half of us were born in this country – we know how things work and that you want to punish the offenders. But why do you think arranging a sausage sizzle is going to solve the problem?'

Councillor Franks tries to answer, but by now everyone is talking. Some of the Year Elevens start sniggering at Councillor Franks until Zayden and his friends give them death stares.

'When my older cousins started uni or their apprenticeships the year after the Cronulla riots,' Zayden continues, 'it was hard for them to get part-time jobs or to get into places because of their ethnicity. After the riots, one of the federal politicians arranged for four boys from Bankstown Boys High to walk the Kokoda Track with a couple of Aussie boys from Cronulla. Others got to go to Gallipoli. You know what they all had in common, Councillor? They were all Lebanese *Muslims*. Not that there's anything wrong with that, but we don't want people coming in here and talking about the efforts they're making for us when only half of our community get to take part in them.'

Franks looks stunned. I feel inspired and stoked that I haven't been crushing on a shallow guy for all these years.

'You go on about how Australia's made up of all different people and communities,' Zayden says, 'but so are we. The Lebanese people aren't just Christian and Muslim, they're also Druze and Jewish. When something bad happens, we all get labelled the same way, but when a good opportunity comes along, only one part of the Lebanese community gets to participate. How come my cousins missed out on the opportunities in 2006, but now you want to invite us to some sister council barbecue? We don't want to hear your thoughts on fairness when you don't practise what you preach.'

Franks glances nervously at his watch. He quickly finishes his talk by telling us about what's going on at council level and leaves the hall.

As everyone starts talking again, I notice Sister Magdalena having a serious conversation with the (very cute) police officer who spoke to us earlier. She turns to face us and claps her hands three times, signalling for us to quieten down.

'Seniors,' she says, dramatically, 'Constable Adam Baldwin has stayed back today to talk to you briefly about a very serious matter. I hope you will assist him if you're able to. As I have told you time and time again, without those who protect us by enforcing the laws that make our society great, we would be in a state of anarchy. If you listen to Constable Baldwin quietly, you may leave early today as a special treat. But I will leave that to Mr Trebold's discretion. Good afternoon, Constable Baldwin.' She's about to leave, then turns back to us with an almost pleading look in her eyes. 'Please behave,' she says, scanning the room. 'All of you!'

Constable Baldwin walks to the centre of the room and clears his throat. I notice a few Year Eleven girls at the front gazing at him admiringly, as if he were Prince Charming come to rescue them from their bored teenage slumber.

When he starts talking about the Brighton brawl, all the slouchers in the hall sit up straight, including Zayden and his friends. I notice Zayden has a defiant look on his face and wonder if he knows something.

Constable Baldwin explains that he's a member of the special Bankstown squad the Commissioner has formed to investigate the violence.

I hear Vanessa whisper to Rita behind me: 'As if they expect us to rat on our own people.'

'Those hooligans who decided to retaliate are the ones causing your lovely culture grief,' Constable Baldwin says, looking undisturbed by the number of death stares directed at him. 'So instead of letting them harm your reputation further, let us deal with them before they get you into even more trouble.'

By now we're evenly divided along an axis of get-out-of-here looks and he-has-a-point shrugs.

Constable Baldwin sighs when no one responds. 'Look, I know this probably feels pretty crappy for you guys,' he says, glancing at Mr Trebold as if worried he's going to be chastised for using the word 'crappy'. 'The recent violence was almost as bad as what happened in Cronulla when you were young – a dark chapter in the history of a country that's always been about embracing others.'

Someone sniggers at the back, but Mr Trebold glares at them and they shut up. Constable Baldwin keeps going.

'As I understand it, a young fellow from this school was injured in the brawl, so you owe it to him that everyone responsible for those stupid acts – no matter which side they were on – is brought to justice. They need to pay for the havoc and pain they've wreaked on our society, on people going about their daily business. I realise you might not want to raise your hands now, so I'm leaving some business cards with Sister Magdalena. I know she'll be very pleased with any effort you make in aiding our investigation. Remember, it's always better to work with us than against us.' And with a tip of his hat, he's gone.

We file out of the hall to see Sister Magdalena waiting for us. She doesn't discipline Zayden for his earlier behaviour – perhaps because she believes that for once in his life he's said something worthwhile.

Dora is way in front of me, and despite the fact that we usually walk out of the school gates together, I don't run to catch up with her. Although I'm still struggling to accept our changing friendship, there isn't much I can do about it. No one stays friends forever, right?

I'm almost at the front of the school when the sight of my brother having a conversation with Zayden stops me in my tracks. They seem to be arguing, like Zayden is trying to convince Andrew of something. It's weird. Apart from the fact that Zayden's cousin George is one of Andrew's good friends, they have nothing in common, and as far as I know they've never spoken.

'Hey, Andrew,' I call out as I approach. 'How come you're out early? Wagging class?'

'No!' he says, a little too quickly.

I sense he's hiding something, but before I can say anything else, Zayden turns to me and smiles.

'Relax, Sophie. Cut the boy some slack.'

I stare at him dreamily, almost forgetting why I'm there. He picks up his school bag and gestures for me to walk alongside him. Andrew gives me a look and walks away.

'What did you think of my performance today?' Zayden asks. 'Pretty good, ay? I love putting people in their place.'

I laugh. 'You did that all right, but there was so much passion behind what you were saying. And you were so right. I was proud of you for sticking up for the boys.'

'Pfft,' he says. 'I don't really give a shit. None of the stuff I said was anything I came up with! My cousin's a journalist and she was going on about it all the other day. I just needed some ammo to back me up when I subtly told the guy to screw it. There's no way in hell we want to be mixing with the kind of scum in the Shire and eastern suburbs – something that our little friend Mr Goldsmith will figure out soon enough.'

He raises his voice for the last part, and I realise Shehadie is walking in front of us, so close he's probably heard the whole thing. Zayden looks at me as though I should be impressed, but before I get a chance to react Vanessa calls out to him to offer him a lift home in her car.

I make my way over to where Mum is waiting, my conversation with Zayden playing over and over in my mind. I can't believe he spoke so powerfully about something he doesn't even care about just to get at Councillor Franks. He made out that he was passionate about the subject, but when it came to the crunch, it was all show. That hurts – especially because what he was arguing about means so much to me.

On our drive home, I see Shehadie walking to his grandma's place. He looks as though he's carrying the weight of the world on his shoulders. For a second, my heart aches for him. I know what it's like to feel invisible, but at least I'm kind of the same as everyone else. The last thing you want to be in high school is different.

I remember what Constable Baldwin said about it being better to work with the cops rather than against them, and I wonder if we should be doing the same thing with Shehadie. After all, it's going to be a long year, and we're all trying to figure out what will happen when we leave our cocoon. Will we flourish or flail in the big wide world?

7

I hate that I still can't
fight my own battles

'Did you know that two out of three children who are denied access to education are girls?' I call out to Leila as I lie sprawled on the floor of her spare room.

She appears in the doorway. 'That's pretty bad, Soph, but does it have any relevance whatsoever to the exam you're studying for?' She raises her eyebrows because she already knows the answer.

I shrug guiltily. 'It's boring! I don't think anyone in my entire year will ever use algebra in their careers, and I am *not* exaggerating.'

She gives me a smirk. 'Be that as it may, you told your mother you needed to come here for some space to study, so study is what you'll do. And, I might add, algebra's going to be in your exam whether it's relevant to your future or not.'

I pout at her and she softens. 'How about a cup of tea? Maybe a five-minute break will do you good.'

A few minutes later, I'm sitting on her sofa, drinking a glass of Milo and eyeing the gorgeous leadlight shade hanging from the ornate ceiling of her living room. Leila and her best friend, Lisa, live in Sylvania, in a beautiful Californian bungalow. Bankstown used to have the same style of houses – until my parents' generation knocked them all down and replaced them with giant wog palaces complete with columns and stone statues in the front yard.

Lisa works shifts, and when she's away I love coming here and hanging out with Leila. Dad usually drops me off in the morning and I get to spend the entire day relishing some downtime.

'So tell me,' Leila says, munching on an Oreo, 'how's the famous Zayden?'

'I dunno,' I mumble.

She gives me a knowing look.

'We were on holidays for ages,' I say, rolling my eyes. 'And I've barely spoken to him since we got back to school. We don't have a lot of classes together.'

'Wasn't there some beach party you were going to? That would've been a good chance to talk to him.'

'It would, had your brother let me go.'

She scrunches up her face in disappointment. 'Aww, no way! Why didn't you call me, kiddo? That's what I'm here for!'

'Meh,' I say. 'I was entirely unfazed.'

She knows I'm lying.

'Was it because of the Brighton Brawl?' she asks. 'If so, I get it, because it could've turned into something nasty.'

'Yeah, but it didn't,' I say, wounded. 'Nothing happened at all. It was just another exciting thing that I missed out on.'

'Aww, little one, you're too young to remember Cronulla, but your dad isn't. He was probably picturing you being mauled by a crowd chanting "No Allah in the Nulla".'

'Yeah, I guess,' I say, my voice trailing off. I'm trying not to cry in front of her. 'I'm not as bummed about not going to the party as I am about Dora going without me. I mean, I know I can't expect her not to go – she's kind of my Zayden spy anyway – but she's been a bit weird ever since. I think it's because she spent the night hanging around Rita Malkoun and Vanessa – you know, the popular girls. She doesn't bitch about them the way she used to, and they're getting really friendly at school and stuff.'

'Is she ditching you for them?'

'No,' I admit. 'It's not like that. Well, not yet anyway. But I'm scared that it will be. I mean, I don't want to be invisible, but I don't really wanna hang out with them either, you know? And she always wants to.' I sigh. 'I wish they'd opened the school to more than just Lebs. I feel so different to everyone else at school, not just because I think about things on a bigger scale, but for other reasons too. I don't cry about my blow-dried hair when it rains, and I don't feel the need to have a boyfriend just to make some sort of cool statement.'

'I hate to tell you this, little one, but most girls are like that. It's not exclusive to high school and it's not exclusive to Lebanese people. You can be your mother's age and still be trying to figure this stuff out.'

We're both silent for a while. For some reason I haven't told her about the new guy at school, even though I normally would.

'You know what the best thing for you would be?' she says. 'A job.'

'A job?' I pull a quizzical face.

'Yeah! You'll get to meet new people outside your school, and some of them won't be Lebanese, so you'll at least get to

60

feel like you're living in Australia. And you'll get to spend some time away from home, even though you'll be at work. It'll stop you going insane.'

'That'd be awesome!' I say. 'Plus, there'll be the added perk of money in my pocket.'

'Tell me about it! How cool would that be?' She claps her hands. 'What kind of place do you picture yourself working at? I worked at McDonald's, then a newsagent. McDonald's was pretty busy, but the newsagent was kind of boring because we only ever got old people buying Lotto tickets on pension day.'

'Erm, before we get too excited, what if my parents say no? I mean, they really want me to focus on getting good marks this year. Mum even takes the phone off the hook when I get home from school because she wants no interruptions when I'm studying.'

'Then we need to figure out a way to convince them it's going to enhance your education in some way,' Leila says, a gleam in her eye. She thinks about it for a second or two. 'What if we tell them that you'll need a casual job when you're at uni, and you're better off getting one now before it gets too competitive? That's true enough, and I reckon my brother would believe it.'

I sit up. 'Yeah, I guess so. But, Leila, he'd embarrass me – he'd want to visit me at work to see that I was okay, or send Mum to wait outside and drive me home as soon as I finish. I wouldn't get to hang out with anyone.'

'Good point,' she admits. 'What if we make it so it's too far out of their way to come collect you?'

'Then they'll just say it's not worth it. It's not like they care about me earning money. They don't expect me to pay board or anything.'

'Another good point.' Then she hits the jackpot. 'I know! My friend Rachel's sister manages the Big W in Miranda. I've met her a few times and she's really nice. What if I ask her to give you a job on the weekends? You can come and sleep here after family dinner on Friday night, then I'll take you back home on Saturday after you finish work?'

'That's an idea with potential,' I say excitedly. Then I scrunch up my face again. 'Except Dad's always saying that good Lebanese girls –'

'Never spend the night anywhere but their father's house until they get married,' she says, finishing the sentence for me. 'Soph, honestly, nobody cares any more. Tonnes of Lebanese girls travel interstate for work these days, or go to hotels for hen's nights or go away on their own. It doesn't mean they're skanky or slutty or whatever that generation think. Your dad needs to get over it – don't worry, I'll talk to him.' She extends her arm to pull me up off the floor. 'Trust me, little one, all will be fine.'

─⁓─

Leila drives me home, muttering under her breath as she psyches herself up to face my dad. Despite the fact that she's his little sister, Leila's probably the only person apart from Mum he'll actually listen to.

I think back to the time Leila got engaged to Peter. She'd argued her case with Dad without any of the wussy crying that usually accompanies my campaigns. I was seven years old at the time, and I'd hidden upstairs when I heard him bellowing about how she was throwing away her culture and history to marry an Asian. He would only accept a Lebanese guy, because it would guarantee that our traditions, 'the safeguards of our lifestyles', would stay intact.

'You see how easy it is for these people to divorce, ya Leila?' he'd yelled. 'What makes you think he won't wake up one day and decide to leave you? By then you might have three kids and you'll have to come crawling back to me, all alone.'

But Leila had been defiant, and I'd decided then and there that she was my hero.

'Don't you get it, Elias?' she'd argued. 'My life would be more comfortable than Mama's ever was! I won't have to hang on his every word because he's the man and gets to run everything.'

Leila meant that she wouldn't have to be a Stepford wife, washing and ironing her husband's clothes, having his dinner warm on his plate when he came home. She'd never have to do the dishes alone after every meal, or spend her time mopping and dusting and cleaning toilets while her husband lay on the couch because that's how it had been done in his family for generations. She hadn't said any of that to Dad, though. Instead, she'd given him a date, a time and a venue and warned him that he'd die of shame if people talked about how he hadn't given her away. And she'd won, because he knew she was right and because he could never say no to her. The wedding didn't happen in the end, but if it had, he'd have walked her down the aisle to make her happy.

Despite Leila's previous successes, I'm not convinced Dad will agree to me working so far away. And when she tells him that it would be a good idea for me to get a job, he just stares at me like she's told him I have a strange genetic mutation that can only be cured by spreading a paste of ground-up goats' horns all over my body.

'Is this true, Sophie?' he asks.

'Yes,' I reply softly.

He turns to Leila. 'Did you put this idea in her head?'

'No, Dad, it's –' I start.

'I'm talking to my sister, Sophie.'

Mum motions for me to be quiet. I make a face at her to indicate she should say something.

'Elias, it's not a big deal, it'll be good for her,' Leila says. 'A lot of people have jobs, you know.'

'Please, Leila, do not insult my intelligence in my own home.' Dad waves his hands at her accusingly.

She folds her arms. 'Well then, why don't you think about it at least? And be realistic. The girl needs to socialise with people who aren't blood relatives. Imagine sending her off to university on her own when she's had zero exposure to the world around her?'

'You and Sophie are constantly making out that I am a prison guard and our heritage is a gaol,' he says, nodding in my direction. 'I make these rules for her own protection. People stab their mothers and rape their daughters in that outside world she wants to be a part of. I am trying to protect her from people who might influence her negatively or harm her.'

Leila starts to argue again, but he cuts her off. 'You of all people should know that, sister,' he says in a low voice.

Mum tugs at his jacket and I wonder what the gesture means.

Dad sighs. 'I don't want Sophie to be miserable, but I know what is acceptable in our community. I know how people think. I can make one phone call to find out if a friend comes from a good family. Once she starts socialising outside, I have no idea who she is with, what effect they might have on her.'

Leila shakes her head. 'It's just a job. Thursday nights and some weekends. I can even help. I'll take her back to mine on Friday nights after dinner, and you can pick her up Saturday afternoons before your cab run.'

He is silent and I can't tell what he's thinking. My stomach clenches in anticipation.

'I don't want her working mid-week,' he concedes finally. 'It might affect her schooling. Sunday should be a family day, but Saturdays should be no problem.'

'Thanks, Dad!' I say, jumping up and clapping my hands.

'I change my mind if I notice your marks are slipping,' he says, pointing a finger at me in warning.

—m—

I spend the next few days relishing the prospect of having a job and a chance to get out of the house on weekends. I'm so grateful to Leila for trying to save me; she's even managed to convince Dad that no store will hire me if I can only work Saturdays and the only solution is to apply to Big W in Miranda, where a good friend of hers is manager.

On Wednesday Leila calls to tell me I'll be starting work in two Saturdays' time – no interview required.

I'm stoked that my barriers are finally coming down and I'm getting a chance to do something different. But something still gnaws at me, undermining my happiness. As I lie awake in bed that night it hits me: I'm seventeen years old and fighting for my freedom, but I've let my aunty do most of the fighting for me. How can I expect to stop being invisible if I'm not brave enough to make myself heard?

8

I hate it when the universe
plays tricks on me

I'm a nervous wreck as Leila drives me to Big W for my first shift. I already know I'm going to make a bad first impression because I'm wearing the ugliest white shirt in the history of humanity. Mum found it for $4.79 on the clearance rack at Best & Less and insisted I wear it, refusing to let me pay $70 for a nicer one from Sportsgirl or Cue. Admittedly, it's not so much hideous as a hideous fit. What I really wanted was something preppy: a fitted shirt with rolled-up sleeves. My lapse in style makes me thankful there's no chance of seeing anyone I know while I'm at work.

Leila parks the car and switches off the ignition. 'Okay, kiddo, time to face the music. Off you go.'

She gestures towards the shopping centre's giant automatic doors. I remain fixed in my seat.

'Geez, what's the matter with you, Soph? You were so excited about this a week ago.'

'Errr, maybe I'm not cut out for this yet. Heaps of people don't get jobs until after school. Maybe I'll just wait,' I say, my eyes pleading with her to turn around and drive us back to her house.

'Are you serious? We spent ages negotiating with Dictator Dad for this! It's settled. We're not going back to him with our tails between our legs.'

'Why can't I just hang out with you every Saturday? We could have fun, talk, do stuff ...' My voice trails off; even I don't know why I'm so scared.

'What about all the money you're supposed to be earning? Or the experience that's going to add value to your education?' she asks. 'I don't do all the solving; you gotta work with me, baby girl. And please don't ever assume I have nothing better to do with my time other than wait around for the likes of you.' She nudges me playfully, but I notice an edge to her voice. 'Now, scoot.'

I know when I'm beaten, so I kiss her on the cheek and climb out of the car. I'm meant to meet with a man named Andre at the front desk at 8.30 am ... in exactly three minutes.

I hurry through the centre to the rolled-down grille over Big W's front doors. I can't find a handle to tug it up with. I must look like an idiot as I pace back and forth staring at the grille, until a blond guy with messy longish hair and pale skin comes up.

'I'm Jordan,' he says. 'Are you new?'

I nod, then find my voice. 'Sophie – first day. Nervous wreck.'

He laughs lightly. 'Don't worry, it's nothing. You'll come to hate it.' He rolls the grille up and motions 'After you', then walks in behind me and closes the door. 'Let me guess – meeting Andre?'

I nod again.

'He's nice, don't worry,' he says, his face relaxing into a smile. 'And even if he wasn't, he delegates everything anyway. You'll probably have someone else doing your intro.'

A few minutes later, I'm standing in a small storeroom that doubles as an office and being asked a load of questions. It's a waste of breath answering them because two minutes later I'm doing it all over again, on forms this time. Andre buzzes for someone to take me around the store and give me the lowdown on staff numbers, trading hours, lunch breaks, and storeroom and delivery locations.

'It's a lot to take in,' Anita, my guide, explains. 'Especially on the first day. The training manager's on leave for a couple of weeks, but we recently appointed an assistant to work with him. The assistant's a casual too and is responsible for babysitting new staff on Saturdays. He'll spend the first three shifts with you until you get the hang of everything. He's really nice and extremely patient. He used to be on the registers, but we figured he'd be better off training newbies because he has a way of making them feel comfortable despite all the overwhelming things they have to learn.'

Forget the first three shifts, I think. I'm having trouble taking in the information that's been fed to me over the last hour, especially now that the store is open and slowly filling with customers.

Anita leads me to another door, and I figure this is the place where I'll meet the assistant training guy. She puts her ear against the door and I look at her questioningly.

'Sorry, that must look weird,' she says. 'He told me earlier that he needed to make a call, so I wanted to see if I could hear whether or not he's done.'

I nod.

'Let's play it safe,' she says. 'Knock on the door in a couple of minutes, he should be done by then. He can start you off with the basics, and before you know it you'll be a pro.' She winks at me and walks off.

'But wait,' I call to her retreating figure. 'I don't even know his name.'

After what feels like ages, I knock and a voice calls out, 'Come in.' I open the door, and the guy inside turns around. To my horror, I find myself face to face with Shehadie Goldsmith.

'What the hell are you doing here?' he says, not bothering to hide his contempt.

'I'm your new trainee,' I say, wishing I could crawl into a hole.

Shehadie and I stare at each other with a mixture of distress, confusion and dismay.

'Well, we'd better get to it then,' he mumbles, pulling an orientation booklet out of a drawer and placing it on the table in front of me. 'Welcome to Big W.'

I smile sarcastically and roll my eyes. How is it that fate can render a person completely and utterly powerless? Like I didn't feel powerless enough as it was.

All morning I feel tortured by Shehadie's presence. Admittedly, after his initial frostiness he's nothing other than polite to me. At lunchtime, he takes me back to the little staffroom.

'You get a half-hour,' he says. 'I recommend you take it here, because if you leave the store you're going to be

69

stopped by customers as you walk in and out, which eats, like, eight minutes of your break time. If you have a book to read, you should go outside – there's a shortcut to avoid the store. Go down this long corridor, take a left and then the second right past the bathrooms.'

'Thanks,' I say awkwardly. I feel bad because I've been so rude to him at school, but he's acting like it's water under the bridge.

'If you need anything from me, just ask,' he says. 'Most of the people you'll be rostered on with are young and really cool, so don't be worried or nervous. I'm sure you'll fit right in. I'll introduce you to some people later, when we're doing end of day.'

'Thanks.'

'No problem,' he says, shaking his head. 'See how much better that makes a new person feel?'

He winks at me as he leaves the room, and I bury my head in my hands.

—⁂—

The day gets worse when I'm put on a register.

After my first few goes with Shehadie supervising, he smiles. 'You're a natural.'

'Gee, thanks. My life is complete – I can successfully scan some barcodes. Round up some awards.'

'Don't use that tone with me, young lady,' he says, as I bag a customer's products and wish her a lovely day. I make a face at him and he laughs. 'Reckon you can do it on your own now?'

'Ummm ...'

'Oh, not so confident now, are we?' he says, poking fun at me. 'Or do you just want me to stick around?'

I shake my head, just as two female staff members walk by holding a large box between them and giggling.

'What are you guys doing?' Shehadie calls out to them.

'Trying to get this over to cosmetics, but someone keeps dropping the box,' one calls back, tilting her head at her friend.

'It's heavy,' the other girl says. 'Plus I got a manicure this morning.'

'Couldn't you get a trolley?' Shehadie asks.

'You know us,' the first girl replies. 'Low on logic, high on fun.'

'Yeah, I bet.' He grins. 'Hold on a sec, I'll be right over.' He puts his hand on my back. 'You okay on your own?'

I shrug. 'I guess so.'

'Two minutes ago you were as cocky as hell with your barcode scanning comment, and now there's two damsels in distress waiting for me and you don't want me to go? I never pictured you as the jealous type.'

I sigh.

'Too early for jokes, huh? Trust me, the days go on forever if you don't have a little fun.'

I smile reluctantly.

'And speaking of fun,' he bows with a flourish, 'duty calls.'

I watch him carry the box effortlessly while the girls fall in alongside him, laughing and flirting, and wonder if it would kill me to be a little less uptight. It's almost like I go out of my way to avoid fun.

My thoughts are interrupted when a woman places her items down on the conveyor belt.

'Hi, how are you today?' I ask as I scan and bag her products.

She ignores me and picks up a magazine, so I raise my eyebrows and continue to scan in silence.

'That'll be $86.50,' I say.

She puts the *New Idea* back in the stand and looks at me like I'm stupid. 'Ah, no, that's not right. Did you scan something twice?'

'I don't think so.'

'You're wearing a trainee badge,' she snaps. 'Of course you did something wrong. I calculated how much it was all going to cost and you've added about $30 extra.'

'I'm sorry, but it's all automatic,' I say. 'Whatever the price is, even if it's on sale, it's calculated automatically at checkout.'

She puts her hands on her hips. 'I don't care. I'm not going to pay that. Why don't you run through every item and we'll see where you've made the mistake?'

I ignore the comment and start checking each item and its cost.

Her hand comes up in front of my face. 'There you go, the sheets,' she says, looking like she's just disproved climate change.

'What about them?' I ask, confused.

'You've charged me $30 extra for the sheets,' she says very slowly, making me want to punch her. 'They're supposed to be $25.'

I flip the pack over and check the price underneath the barcode. It says $55. I scan it: $55.

'Ma'am, they're labelled and scanning as $55,' I say. 'I can't charge you $25 for them. Where did you see them for $25?'

'Are you insinuating something?' she asks, raising her voice.

'Not at all. I just don't understand why you thought they were $25. Just trying to help.'

'You're not trying to help,' she says, death-staring me. 'You're calling me a liar. I saw them for $25.'

'No,' I stammer. 'I'm just trying to work out this misunderstanding.'

'I'll tell you where the misunderstanding is. Legally, you're obliged to give them to me for the price I saw – $25.'

I feel cornered. I take a deep breath. 'I hope you don't mind, but I'll just have to confirm that. As you said, I'm new, and I need to make sure I take the appropriate measures.'

The customers behind her wander off to other registers and I start to panic.

'Look, I really don't appreciate you trying to rip me off,' she says angrily.

'Ma'am, I'm not trying to rip you off. Let me call a supervisor and sort this out for you.'

'You do that,' she says, making a face at me. 'Your kind are all about cheating the system, but there's no way in hell that I'm going to let you cheat me.'

Shehadie looks over from the cosmetics department and senses my panic. He's with us in seconds. 'Hi,' he says, smiling at the customer. 'Is there a problem here?'

'Your trainee is making things difficult for me,' the woman says, glaring at me.

'Oh, I'm sure that's not her intention,' he says. 'She's just new.'

I explain the situation to him without repeating her racist remark.

'How about I send someone over to check it out?' he asks, attempting to placate her.

He pages the manchester department, and a woman in her mid-twenties comes over. They have a chat, and she leaves and returns with an identical pack of sheets.

'I'm sorry, madam, but there's been a misunderstanding,' Shehadie says. 'Someone's placed those sheets with the cheaper ones. They're a different pattern and thread count, and further down the aisle you can see that they're shelved where they're supposed to be.'

She narrows her eyes at him. 'But legally you're supposed to charge me the cheaper price because that's what they're labelled.'

'Actually, they're labelled $55,' he says. 'And this pack is the only one that wasn't in its section. If they were all there, it would have been our fault.'

'But you should still charge me the lower price. It's not my fault.'

'Well, it's not ours either, and it's against store policy. It's also not in line with the Trade Practices Act of 1974 –'

'Fine,' she says in a huff. 'I'll just pay what I owe, except for the sheets. You can keep those.'

My face burns as I swipe her card and hand it back to her with her goods. 'Have a nice day,' I say with a smile she probably wants to rip off my face.

'Well, that was awkward,' Shehadie says after she's gone.

'Awkward for you?' I ask incredulously. 'While you were over there flirting with those girls, I had to put up with her whingeing and racism. She had the hide to talk about "my kind".'

'Oooh, your kind?' he says, making fun of me. 'Do you need to have a lie-down? Was it too much for you to bear? Lucky I'm here to save you now.'

'You're not going to let me live this down, are you?'

'Probably not,' he says, laughing. 'But you might want to learn not to take everything I say seriously. For example, the Trade Practices Act of 1974 is a real federal law, I just have no idea what it means.'

He shrugs and heads over to the front desk, leaving me smiling.

9

I hate it when people find
a way inside my head

Before I know it, first term of school is over and it's the Easter break. My Easter weekend will be filled with church, prayer and a big family feast at my great-aunt's house on the Saturday, complete with about sixty relatives and friends.

On Saturday morning, my sisters and I boil eggs and paint them for our annual egg fight and breakfast on Easter Sunday.

'How come Andrew's not painting with us this year, Sophie?' Marie asks. She looks so cute with her unkempt hair and paint-smeared face that I want to grab her and cover her with cuddles and kisses.

'We have a gender imbalance in our household, Marie,' Angela says. 'Which basically means that because we're girls, we have to stay at home and learn the art of home-making.'

'What do you mean?' Marie says, looking confused.

'What Ang is trying to say is that Andrew doesn't think he has to explain why he doesn't want to join in with us because he's a boy,' I say. 'Dad says that you shouldn't ask a man where he's going, because it's his right to make

76

his own decisions. We're the ones that society expects to behave.'

'Who cares?' Viola says. 'It means one less person in the egg fight, so one of us is more likely to win.'

'True, the silver lining,' Angela agrees.

Mum comes into the kitchen and surveys our work. 'Wow, very pretty eggs from my very pretty girls,' she says. 'But none from my handsome little man this year?'

'Nope,' I say sarcastically. 'Andrew's too good for family traditions.'

But then I feel bad, because Mum looks upset. I can tell that she's thinking about us growing up too fast, and that soon enough we'll stop doing things together because family activities of any kind will be uncool.

Halfway through the second week of the holidays, Dora turns up at our house unannounced.

'Hey, girl,' she says, when I open the door. 'I desperately need your help with my English essay. You're the only one who understands what these loser texts are about.'

I frown. 'Dora, I already explained this assignment to you on the day we got it – three weeks ago! You want to start working on it now? It's due in five days.'

She shrugs. 'I can write it in five days, especially with your help.'

I sigh and open the door wider to let her inside. 'We'll work in the study room. Mine's messy because I'm working on my methodology for my detention centre project. I've printed out a zillion newspaper articles.'

'At least you're making some progress. Gotta do something when all you do is sit at home hanging out with your sisters, right?'

'One, I actually like hanging out with my sisters,' I tell her. 'Most of the time anyway. And two, I've been working at Big W a lot these holidays, at least three times a week.'

'Wow,' she says, setting her stuff down on the table in our study, 'I had no idea you were working so much. I thought your dad had a rule.'

'Mum managed to convince him to let me work extra. Which you'd know if you ever called me for anything other than help with your school work.'

She looks guilty and I let her, because I hate feeling used and it's getting ridiculously obvious that I'm not important in her life right now.

'Sorry, Soph,' she says after a moment. 'I didn't mean to neglect you. I was actually going to ask you if you wanted to go shopping for cruise outfits on Saturday?'

'Can't,' I say. 'Working.'

I've come to love being away from my niche in Bankstown while I'm at work. Most of the locals in Miranda are Anglos or third-generation wogs, so it's a chance to experience a world away from home, even if it's just another Sydney suburb.

'Oh.' Dora looks deflated. 'What if we go Sunday then? Just here at Bankstown?'

I shrug. 'Sure. But let's get cracking on this assignment. Mum and I have a girls night with the aunties and cousins tonight and I have loads to do before we go.'

—◊◊◊—

Leila's right about my job: it feels great to push myself outside of my comfort zone. I even start to feel more confident about my style thanks to the new shirt I bought from Cue with my first pay. By my second month at work, I've mastered the registers, am able to help customers without stopping what I'm doing, and make sure I always get my half-hour lunch break no matter how busy we are. I've also started to make a few friends, people in their late teens and early twenties who are working to save some money before they start uni.

I'm stacking the stationery shelves with Casey Bennett, one of the prettiest girls I've ever seen, when she invites me to her eighteenth.

'I'm sorry, Case,' I say. 'But I'm afraid I can't come.'

'Aww, Soph, I'm gutted!' she says. 'How come you never come out anywhere with us?'

'It's too embarrassing to be seen with someone who's such a grub,' I laugh, wiping the dust from the back of her pants when she stands up to stretch. 'You look like a hobo, Case.'

She knows I'm joking. Casey has dark hair against super pale skin, and her face is a stunning mix of amazing green eyes, high cheekbones and a really cute button nose peppered with freckles. But most of all, she's slim with long legs and little curves in all the right places.

She pokes her tongue out at me as she grabs another stack of notepads to pile on the shelf. 'My birthday's in two months. I'm giving you plenty of notice, so there's no reason why you can't make it.'

'Case, need I remind you again how many relatives I have and the number of parties and dinners that translates to?' I say. 'Sometimes I have more weddings in a season than some people have in their entire lives.'

'Hence the two months' notice,' she says.

I exhale, caught between new friendship and old rules.

'Seriously, come on,' she says. 'Last week, Jordan told me that you turned down coffee with the Sunday School Crew three times in a row. They startin' to think you hatin' on them, girl,' she says, gangsta style.

The Sunday School Crew are a bunch of high school kids who're always rostered on Sundays because the uni students are too hungover. I only work some Sundays, but I still feel like part of the group. I'd always assumed they weren't bothered by me turning down invitations, but clearly that isn't true.

'It's because she secretly hates me,' a voice says behind us. We turn around to see Shehadie. 'She has to deal with me every single day at school, and then on weekends I get to be her boss.'

Casey laughs. 'Ah yes, the Lebanese school in Bankstown,' she says. 'I didn't know you went there, Soph.'

'Anyway, girls, as your supervisor I feel I need to point out that you're doing it all wrong. You're supposed to do it like this.'

He grabs a stack of notebooks from Casey's hands and dumps the whole lot on top of us, laughing like a thirteen-year-old. His smile is infectious and shows a set of perfect white teeth.

Casey glances at her watch. 'Well, she's gonna hate you even more now, Goldsmith, because I'm only rostered on till four, which means she has to restock these shelves by herself.'

And with a dramatic curtsy, she's out of there, leaving Shehadie and me to deal with a messy pile of notebooks and two full boxes of stationery.

'So, you wanna thank me for saving you or what?' he says.

'You have to be the most arrogant, presumptuous and self-centred person I've ever met,' I say, straightening a pile of exercise books before slotting them into place on the shelf.

'Thank you,' he says, grinning.

'Casey was just bagging me out for not going anywhere with the team,' I admit, trying not to meet his gaze.

'Uh-huh. And?'

'And it's not like I don't want to, but things are a bit complicated right now. It's difficult.'

'Parents giving you a hard time?'

'Do you read minds or something?' I ask, looking at him curiously.

'Oh, that's only half the extent of my power,' he replies, smirking.

I sigh.

'Want to talk about it?' he asks, serious now.

'Not really,' I say. 'You wouldn't understand anyway.'

'Fair enough. But you'd be surprised. It must be something similar to what Mum went through when she wanted to marry my dad. Dad says it was a big taboo. I may not know much about Lebanese culture, but it seems there are loads of rules and regulations, which I'm slowly figuring out thanks to moving in with my grandparents.'

'So this is all new for you?' I ask.

'Yeah, definitely. Like I had no idea that you make certain sweets at Easter time, and a particular meal for Saint Joseph's feast day, and all this other stuff. My mum didn't keep that up … or any traditions really.'

I nod. 'I wonder if she missed it. I think I would. I find lots of things annoying, but I love all that stuff.' I shrug. 'All the cultural traditions. I think they're beautiful.'

'It's so different being with my grandparents,' he admits. 'Tayta and Pop wake up, they have their Lebanese coffee with the lady next door, then Tayta spends half the day preparing some meal that takes lots of effort, making little balls for soups – dumplings and pastries and stuff. Either my mum was lazy, or she didn't learn all that stuff before she married my dad. She couldn't learn it after, because she didn't talk to my grandparents for a long time.'

'What about church?' I ask. 'Did she go to a Maronite church? Have Lebanese friends?'

'We never went to church as a family unless there was a wedding or something,' he explains. 'She went to the Roman Catholic church near our house sometimes; there was no Lebanese – sorry, Maronite – church near us. It wasn't really part of our lives like it is to some of you guys at school. I guess it's a bit cultural as well – like, your festivities and things tie into the religion.'

'I've never thought of it that way, but it makes sense. So is it a real pain being at CSC?'

'It's a massive adjustment, that's for sure,' he says, looking down. I can tell he feels gutted that no one has given him a chance. 'But at least I get to come back here for work every weekend. It means I see less of my friends though. But even if my mum hadn't died ...' He pauses. 'Well, it's been hard moving from Cronulla, where I surfed with my mates every morning, to a place where I'm an outsider.'

He gets up and holds out his hand to pull me up, but I get up on my own instead. For some reason, I'm thinking about what Zayden would say if he saw me take Shehadie's hand.

I follow him out of the stationery aisle towards the storeroom, thinking about how relaxed he is. If I'd gone through half the stuff he's been through, I don't know how I would've reacted.

'You know what? You can still be an outsider even when you're a hundred per cent Lebanese,' I say. 'Just by thinking differently, or wanting to live a little differently, break with some of the social norms. There are things my parents believe that I'll never understand, but I still have to follow them because everyone in our community thinks the same way. If I didn't, people would gossip and I'd bring shame on me and my sisters.'

'I guess my mum was lucky she never had sisters,' he says. 'Eloping with an Aussie bloke just brought shame on her and her parents.'

'You're being sarcastic,' I say.

'Ah, yeah. But attitudes like that get to me, you know. I guess it was a different time back then, and a lot of other things had happened to her family too.'

I nod, not sure what to say.

'You know, you should try to change things with your family while you can,' he says after a moment. 'If they're too strict, you should talk to them. If you think something's bull, you have a right to express it. Otherwise it'll eat away at you and you'll end up like my poor mum, who didn't speak to her parents until I was born. They just couldn't hack that she'd moved away from them, their culture, everything that they wanted her to love.'

I shake my head. 'If I had the opportunity to run, Shehadie, I would. You can trust me on that. It's not like anyone would notice if I disappeared anyway.'

I mutter the last part under my breath, but he must have heard because he says, 'You're not as smart as I think you are, then. Having parents who love and care for you is a great thing and you don't even know it. You just need to work out how to manage their love and over-protectiveness to live the life you want.'

'Don't presume to know anything about my life,' I scoff, turning away.

He grabs my arm and pulls me to face him. 'I'm serious, Soph. I see you in class, and it's obvious what you're thinking, what you're about. You're blessed in a way that you don't understand. If you really hate all this over-dramatised race and assimilation bullshit in the media, you're in a perfect position to do something about it. You're young, smart, and you obviously have enough passion to make people listen. You're more open-minded than most of the people in that school. And I know you write well because you always get complimented on that in class. Your ideas are usually good ...'

I open my mouth to say something, but he continues: '... and I suspect that you already know all this, because underneath your anger I see little bursts of social awareness that, sadly, most people our age seem to lack.'

My face is burning, but still he goes on.

'You have the best of two worlds – Lebanese and Australian. You speak two languages and balance two lifestyles. Maybe you can use that richness to show both communities that it's possible to be at ease with one another?'

I pick up a stack of boxes and blow my fringe out of my face. 'You're lucky you belong in this bright and sunny Shire world that greets you every morning when you go for a surf. Because despite the fact that I live in two worlds, I don't belong in either. I'm too liberal for my Lebanese community and too ethnic for the Aussies. And if no one takes any notice of me now in either world, they sure as hell aren't going to give a shit if I start championing ideas about how we can coexist in harmony.'

And before he can say anything else, I turn my back on him and walk away.

10

I hate being the one who always misses out

On the first week back after the Easter holidays, our school holds its annual fundraising harbour cruise. The senior classes – Years Ten, Eleven and Twelve – get to organise it, and we invite the same grades from a few surrounding Catholic schools. The nuns think the weeks leading up to the cruise are an opportunity for us to spend our time baking cakes, selling chocolates and holding car-wash days 'in commemoration of Christ's suffering', but most of us are just excited about the dance itself and the chance to meet new people to pash and/or go out with.

I decide to put my cynical, anti-social self aside and get a little enthusiastic about the cruise. I plan to join a bunch of girls to get ready at Rita's house, not because I really want to, but because Dora is going and I'm doing everything I can to hold on to the last vestiges of our friendship.

Dad gives me $150 towards a new outfit, then makes a point of telling me how peaceful things can be between us. I want to tell him that I know he's only letting me go because it's an official school function and teachers will be there, but I don't want to start another argument that will only end with me staying at home and stuffing vine leaves with my mother.

Dad drops me off at Rita's house on Friday night. 'Long time since you come here, ay, baba?' he says, leaning against the steering wheel to peer up at the Malkouns' large white-brick home.

'Yeah, it's been a while,' I say quietly. 'But, you know, I've been busy with work and school and stuff.'

I doubt he buys the excuse, but he leans over and kisses my forehead.

'Have fun tonight and be safe on that boat,' he warns, wagging his finger at me. 'No mischief. That boat is carrying my most precious cargo.'

I laugh and he smiles. 'Thanks, Dad. The cruise finishes at twelve, so by the time the Lebanese people learn how to get off the boat in a coordinated fashion, I should be home around one.'

I walk into Rita's giant house and greet her mother like a good Lebanese daughter, then follow the girlish squeals and loud hip-hop music to Rita's room. Inside, clothes, shoes and school backpacks are strewn everywhere, and clutch purses are laid out on a chaise longue by the window. Three girls are crowded around Rita's dressing table mirror, while Rita and Dora are huddled at the mirrored door of her built-in closet, carefully applying lip gloss. Dora looks up as I walk in, and then all the squealing focuses on me.

'You look hot, Soph!'

'Check out her shoes, they're just divine!'

'Soph, girl, I never knew you had legs like that – where you been hiding them?'

I giggle nervously, unused to the attention, but before I know it they're back to their own looking-hot agendas. Only Dora and Rita stay to analyse my make-up – or lack thereof.

'Dude, love the outfit,' Rita says, looking me up and down, 'but the make-up's all wrong. No offence.'

I mean it when I say, 'None taken.' I'm already out of my element in a black PU mini, fishnet stockings, black pointy high heels, and a fitted three-quarter-sleeve top. Dora insisted I buy it on our recent shopping excursion because it 'reveals that you are indeed a female who possesses some boobs'. I'm used to jeans, tees and Converse sneakers, but I have to admit that I'm a little pleased by my reflection in the mirror, even if I've managed to make an otherwise sexy outfit look demure. I've even brought along a jacket for good measure.

'You look totally hot, Sophie,' Vanessa says across the room. 'I mean it. But I just have to know – is your skirt one size too big? Not that it's obvious, but I tend to notice these things.'

'Um, yeah, I wanted it to be a tiny bit longer and looser so I'd feel comfortable dancing in it,' I reply.

Her facial expression says everything and I shake my head in amusement.

'Sophie seems to relish hiding herself from the world,' Dora says, death-staring me.

'Not that Marilyn Monroe has ever been my guide to life or anything,' I say, 'but she said your clothes need to be tight enough to show you're a woman, but loose enough to show you're a lady. And I want to be lady.'

'I like that,' Vanessa says. 'Might get it printed onto one of her pictures and hang it in my room. I have a collection.'

'I bet you do,' I say, smiling sarcastically. Thankfully she doesn't notice. Probably because all the eyeliner she's applied has clouded her vision.

But eyeliner must be some sort of party prerequisite, because suddenly I have girls swarming all over me with brushes and applicators. Amanda starts applying bronzer (ignoring my plea of 'not a lot, because I don't want to look like an LA bimbo') and Rita nearly blinds me while attempting to apply liquid liner (which is pointless anyway, because I have no idea you're supposed to wait for it to dry and rub my eyes straight away because they're itchy). After that nobody's interested in fixing me up any more and I'm grateful to be left alone.

The Hummer limousine arrives and we all storm outside. Even though driving around in a Hummer is the ultimate western-suburbs cliché, I feel special for a second and join in the screaming and screeching all the way to the wharf.

As we're standing around waiting to be security-checked and admitted onto the boat, I'm suddenly aware of being watched. I look up and spot Shehadie and Daniel Abboud talking to each other, ignoring the pushing and shoving around them. Shehadie has his hands in his pockets, while Daniel's animated hand gestures tell me he's talking about his biggest passion: gaming.

I check out Shehadie and am surprised. He's wearing jeans, hung low in the same surfer-dude style he wears his Big W pants, a checked shirt rolled up to his elbows, and Converse Chucks in white. For once, he isn't hiding behind his Prada glasses, messy hair and that bulldog jumper he's so attached to. The Clark Kent in him has suddenly become kind of Superman-ish and I find myself thinking him attractive, much to my chagrin.

I realise he's staring back at me, and it seems like he wants to smile, but we're both out of our element so we just exchange nods and look away.

'That Goldsmith kid's a bit hot, isn't he?' Vanessa says. 'Maybe by the end of the year Zayden will be over hating him and I can go there.'

'Oh, you're such a little minx!' one of her friends says.

I just stare at Vanessa, gobsmacked. 'Why can't you go there now?' I ask, ignoring Dora's second death stare for the night.

Vanessa looks at me like I'm a poor unfortunate puppy. 'Sophie, clearly you have no idea what it's like to be popular. If I talk to him, the rest of the class will think it's okay to talk to him too, and Zayden will be mad. We agreed to keep him at arm's length, to send a message that what's been done to us recently is not okay.'

'Right,' I say awkwardly, while inside I'm wondering what the hell is wrong with them.

On board, the decorations committee have done a great job. I'm not surprised, given the committee is made up of the type of girls who wear heels just to go to the local shopping centre. Dora tugs at my jacket and gestures to a group across the room. I forget Shehadie as soon as I spot Zayden. He's in dark jeans and a fitted polo shirt, laughing with his friends and oblivious to the fact that he's setting hearts aflutter all around the room.

The DJ starts the night off with Bruno Mars' 'Locked Out of Heaven' and soon everyone is dancing. Zayden comes over to our group and starts chatting. I wonder what Dora has told Rita and Vanessa because I hear them saying something to Zayden about me. He glances over at me and smiles.

'Looking good, Sophie.' He gives a long and exaggerated nod. Then he sticks out his arm and says, 'Shall we?' and before I've had a chance to think we're walking towards the dance floor.

'Take off your jacket, you nun!' Dora hisses at me.

We dance to a couple of songs, but he doesn't pay me much attention, and a short time later he goes to dance with another group. I watch him flirt with a couple of girls from another school and feel crushed, even though I know he'd never be interested in me.

Shehadie wanders over and I knows he's seen me staring.

'Really, Sophie?' he asks.

'I don't know what you're talking about.'

'I thought you were against clichés, and yet it's obvious that you have an eye for one particular cliché.'

'Please stop pestering me,' I plead. 'You'll ruin the first good night I've had in ages.'

He makes a face. 'Well, I don't want to do that.'

'Go away then.'

'I'm just a little puzzled, that's all,' he adds softly.

'And why's that?'

He leans over and whispers, 'You're not exactly Queen of Hearts material with all that cynicism, sarcasm and sometimes even bitterness, so it's unlikely the Prom King's going to pick you.'

'Okay, what the hell is your problem?' I say, wanting to kill him with my bare hands. 'What gives you the right to make assumptions about who I do or don't like, and whether or not I'm anyone's type?'

I realise that I'm swearing more in this conversation than I ever have in my whole life.

'I'm just saving you the mortification of finding out that you don't belong with him, and he wouldn't care for you much even if you did. Plus, you're better than him.'

'This conversation is so out of line! Who do you think you are, talking to me like this?'

'Hey, forgive me for hitting a sore spot. But isn't that the Lebanese way of doing things – act first, think later?'

He makes another face at me and walks away, hands in his pockets. I take a loud breath and inch closer to the girls. They don't seem to have noticed anything. Of course, they wouldn't – not with boys from other schools around.

The boat docks at eleven thirty, and it's about a quarter to twelve by the time we're back on the wharf. I've made arrangements to go home with the girls I came with, but we've lost each other in our scramble back to dry land. I spot them with a group of boys and make my way over. My feet are aching and I curse myself for wearing heels.

The group are discussing whether or not they should go to the Star Casino, which is across the road, or to Newtown, where some guy that Vanessa likes works at a pub. Half of them are underage so I wonder why they're bothering, but don't say anything. Instead, I stand there freaking out about how I'm going to get home. Dora is standing on the edge of the group, like she's caught between popularity and our friendship. I try to catch her eye, but she looks away.

'So, are we going?' I ask, breaking the silence. I shiver, hoping someone will say that it's cold and we should go home, but no one does.

Just then, Jason Makdessi rounds the corner in his mother's Toyota Land Cruiser and pulls up at the kerb. 'Come on, guys!' he hollers, sticking his head out of the sun roof. 'Are we gonna check out Saade's new boyfriend or not?'

Vanessa giggles into her (real) fur stole and calls out, 'Stop it!' in a way that indicates she actually doesn't want him to.

I can see that she's loving the attention. As much as I want to tell her that the guys are just looking for something to do and really couldn't care less about the latest object of her affection, I remain silent. I'm still holding out hope they'll decide to go home so I can avoid calling Dad and have him drive all the way over here to pick me up, only to lecture me about the importance of keeping good company for the half-hour ride home.

They decide on Newtown and everyone starts to clamber into the car. Dora and I linger behind. Rita motions to us and Zayden calls out, 'Come on, girls! It's after-party time!'

Dora looks at me pleadingly. 'Can't you tell your dad the boat was delayed?'

'Are you for real? He knows it's a school function and it won't go later than midnight. Besides, if I tell him there's a problem with the boat he's going to come down anyway.'

'But everyone's going ...'

'So what? We've spent the last four years mocking people who do what everybody else does.'

'Yeah, while secretly wishing we were like them,' she points out, looking away.

But I know I've struck a chord so I keep going. I desperately need to win here. 'You seriously can't be thinking of going with them? What if you get busted at the pub for being underage? And don't even get me started on Makdessi's driving! I'm pretty sure it wasn't Pepsi he was guzzling from that hip flask earlier.'

She glances from me to the car. 'Wait up, guys!' she calls out, then turns back to me and whispers, 'I'm sorry, Sophie. But you know how it is.'

And then they're driving off, leaving me standing alone on a Sydney street at five minutes to midnight in fishnets and high heels, tears welling in my eyes.

11

I hate it when things don't go according to plan and I'm the one in the firing line

I don't know what to do. I start walking up towards the Maritime Museum to see if I can spot a taxi at the intersection near the Pyrmont Bridge Hotel. I stand by the doors of the hotel, where there are more people, naively thinking there's less of a chance that some dropkick will start harassing me here.

The dropkick manifests in the form of a bearded thirty-something man who calls to me from inside, where he's sitting on a bar stool. He's covered in tattoos, holds a beer in one hand and has ugly stains on his navy singlet and white boardies. When I see him coming towards the door I freak out.

'Dad,' I call. 'There you are!' I walk away with as much purpose as I can muster, despite the obvious fear in my voice.

I go back towards the Star Casino, and then cross the road and sit on a bench, staring at the water. By now it's 12.05 am and I have no idea what to do. I want to call Dad, who's expecting me home in fifty-five minutes, but at the same time I know it would reduce my already limited chances of ever going out again down to zero.

When I hear footsteps behind me, I'm sure the dropkick has followed me and that I'm going to die in the type of clothes I wear once a year. I'll be forever remembered as the seventeen-year-old who was found dead across from the casino in fishnet stockings and with panda eyes.

'My dad just went to get the car,' I blurt out, afraid to turn around.

'Well then, I guess he won't mind if I wait around and keep you company until he comes back,' Shehadie says as he plops himself down beside me.

My face goes bright red. 'What are you doing here? I thought everyone went home.'

'They did. I saw you as I was driving by, so I parked the car – illegally, I might add – to see if you're okay. Clearly I'm a better knight in shining armour than that loser your eyes kept following tonight.'

I ignore him and stare straight ahead.

'So,' he says after a minute, making a point of looking around, 'where's Mr Kazzi?'

'I'm about to call him,' I say, sighing as I pull out my phone.

His hand reaches out to stop me. 'No way, it's late. I'll take you home.'

'Ah, thanks, but I think the heart attack would be less severe if I ran away to Vegas and became a showgirl rather than turning up in some guy's car.'

Shehadie laughs out loud. 'You are one f'd up chick, you know.'

'Don't swear in the presence of a lady, thank you.'

'First of all, Miss Smarty Pants, I didn't swear, I merely alluded to it. And second of all, since when did ladies walk around late at night in fishnet tights?'

'I'll have you know that once upon a time, the femme fatale look was the height of glamour and was not complete without a pair of fishnet stockings. I'm merely recreating a trend for the modern era.'

But I'm still self-conscious enough to pull my skirt down as much as possible while staring straight ahead.

'At least you have the legs to pull them off,' he says.

My face goes red again and I glare at him.

'Relax, it's not like I wanted to give you a compliment,' he says. 'I assure you it came out involuntarily.'

'The truth has a way of coming out,' I say smugly.

After a moment, I become aware of how quiet it is. I stare at the dark, foreboding water, which, strangely enough, feels more inviting than my current situation. God, why did I have to walk up to the stupid Pyrmont Bridge Hotel? I should have waited for the teachers – I could've gotten a lift with one of them at least, instead of rocking up in the car of the boy I love to hate.

'So,' he says, looking straight at me.

'What? What is it you want to say now, you big pain in the arse?'

He rolls his eyes. 'It's getting cold, Soph. We're both working tomorrow. And we both know that despite the fact that you're trying to convince us otherwise, your dad isn't going to magically turn up here. And you're not going to ring him for reasons I'm not going to attempt to figure out.'

I try to interrupt, but he's on fire.

'I'm also pretty sure that the unicorns stop flying at midnight, so that transportation option is out of the question. So would you please cut me some slack, assume I'm not going to kill you, despite the service I'd be doing to men everywhere, and get in my car so we can both go home?'

I'm defeated. 'I'm not allowed to ride in cars with boys,' I admit.

'Even ones who don't want to get in your pants?' he asks, bewildered.

I raise my eyebrows and stare at him with a 'did-you-just-go-there' look on my face.

'I say inappropriate things when I'm ready to hang out at the *Farshi* Club with DJ Pillow and the blanket crowd,' he says almost shyly.

'Ha, you said an Arabic word!' I laugh. 'Well done!'

'A girl in Year Eleven was giving me lessons out on the deck when Daniel went to take a leak,' he explains. 'I forgot to ask her name, so now I'm going to be the Aussie With Bad Manners at school, because just being the Aussie clearly wasn't enough.'

I smile at him in spite of myself. 'Surely your new knowledge of the Lebanese language will help in that department?'

'You think there's hope for me after all?' he asks.

'Perhaps.'

'So are we leaving or what?' he says. 'I don't know about you, but I'd like to get home before the sun comes up to avoid giving my tayta a heart attack.'

I look at him, a pained expression on my face. It's a lose-lose situation.

'Look, if you're really not allowed in cars with boys,' he says, 'I'll stop a few houses away so your dad won't see the car even if he's awake. And I'll tell my tayta and pop to say they picked us up if he does find out anything, okay?'

I'm still quiet, staring at a piece of gum on the ground.

He shakes my shoulder, then bends down and sticks his face under mine, pretending to analyse my expression. 'Sophie, it's quarter past twelve.'

I relent. 'Okay. But do you think you can get me home by 1 am? I kind of have a curfew.'

As we walk towards the car, I say, 'Don't tell your grandparents to lie on my behalf. If my parents ask, I'll just have to deal with it. And don't you dare speed, or try any funny business either.'

'Geez, you have a lot of demands for someone who needs a favour,' he says. He turns around and makes a show of walking in the opposite direction. 'Think maybe you can walk home instead?'

I grab his arm and steer him back to the line of cars. 'Find your car, get in it and drive me home, Goldsmith,' I say.

'Yes, miss.' He salutes me mockingly, then mutters 'Women' under his breath, just as I am rolling my eyes and saying 'Men'.

We catch each other out and both grin.

—⁓—

On the drive home, I ask about his car – a green Holden Commodore and a fairly recent model for someone who's only eighteen.

'I love Holdens,' he says. 'They're like the quintessential Aussie bloke car, don't you reckon?'

I shrug, because I genuinely have no idea, and he smiles.

'I've been working since I was fifteen, and when I got my Ps I didn't want to drive around in some dodgy old bomb. So Dad and I made a deal that he'd pay for half the car if I came up with the other half, plus the costs for rego and insurance. It was a pretty good deal.'

'I bet. You must have been really disciplined.'

He slides a look at me. 'Yeah, well, when I really want something, I'm not the type of person to let anything get in my way.'

I laugh, and realise how safe and comfortable I feel for someone who ought to be freaking out about breaking her strict father's rules. That is until we start fighting over the stereo. For a Shire guy, Shehadie's taste in music is surprisingly Bankstown. He raps along (really badly) to a hip-hop playlist on his iPod while I attempt to turn the radio to something like Triple J or 2DAY FM in the hope of finding some soft rock.

'Look, there's nothing black, ghetto or gangsta about you,' I say. 'So stop pretending to be something you're not, and stop rapping to Kanye before you permanently damage my ears.'

'For the love of God!' he says, gripping the steering wheel tighter. 'Now I can't listen to rap and hip hop because I'm too white? Is there anything I'm allowed to do around you people? Half of me *is* Lebanese, you know?'

I pull my hand off the stereo control. 'Geez, no need to get so haughty.'

'Why are you into all that pop rock alternative shit anyway?' he asks. 'How come you're not into the same music as all your little friends?'

'I like angsty and melodramatic music,' I say. 'It's good for all the soap-opera issues I have going on inside my head.'

He laughs. 'And doesn't that say a lot?'

I smirk at him, and we drive the rest of the way in a comfortable silence.

He pulls up three doors down from my house. I'm relieved to see that the light in the downstairs living room isn't on, which means Dad has decided not to wait up for me. I say thank you to Shehadie and tiptoe into the house. Despite how bad I was feeling just an hour ago, I have to admit the night hasn't been a total disappointment.

—〰—

'Sophie, who did you come home with last night?' Dad asks at the breakfast table the next morning.

Oh, shit.

'Elias, it's 7 am. Do you really need to have this conversation with her now?' Mum asks. 'She looks half-asleep and she has to work all day.'

Listen to your wife! the voice in my head yells. *Listen to your wife!*

But Dictator Dad is still waiting for an answer.

'My friends, Dad,' I say, trying to keep my cool. 'Like I said I would.'

'Are you friends with boys now?' he asks. 'Riding with them all alone in the dark, then getting them to drop you off a few houses down so I can't see you? As if you have something to hide?'

'The lights were off and so I assumed everyone was asleep.' *Including you.* 'I didn't want the car headlights to shine into the house and wake everyone up.'

'But you said you were coming home with the girls,' he persists.

'Well, it didn't work out, Dad. In the end there were too many of us, so we took lifts with other people. But we all drove behind each other so that if something happened we'd be close by.'

'Why didn't Dora come home with you?' he asks. 'Did you especially want to be alone with that boy? And how come he has such a big new car for such a young boy?'

'*Bayii*,' I say through gritted teeth, 'I'm home safe, okay? That's all that matters. I didn't fit in the car with the girls, so I was offered a lift with my friend Shehadie. I don't know why he drives that car. I'm not nosey, unlike every other member of the Lebanese population here in Sydney.'

'Sophie, don't talk about your people like that,' Angela says, walking into the room and giving me a mocking smile.

'I'm going to clobber you, you know that?' I say. But Dad is still waiting for an answer. I sigh. 'What were you doing spying on me anyway? I thought you were asleep.'

'No, I was awake. I was watching through the downstairs window for you to come home.'

'With the lights off?' I ask, incredulous. 'Why can't you just trust me? I'm not going to do anything wrong. I know your rules and I've never broken them.'

'Well, obviously last night you didn't deserve to be trusted.'

Mum shoots him a look. 'That's not what your father's saying. He's just worried because if you're not dropped off in the driveway, it looks suspicious. People in the street will think that we don't know you're going to be home late, or who you're coming home with. We're just trying to protect your reputation.'

'I can't believe this,' I say. 'Any other daughter would have lied. Some girls even went out after the cruise. Why can't you be grateful that I came home and didn't lie to you? Why can't you get that I'm a good girl and give me a chance?'

'Because good girls would ring and ask their father first!' Dad exclaims. 'And good girls would not have been out to begin with. And good girls don't get dropped off around the corner so that the neighbours think they have something to hide and start gossiping about them.'

'*Bayii*, I thought I was doing a good thing,' I plead. 'Especially because it was a school function, not any ordinary event. Plus, every girl I know is allowed to go out more than I am. Lebanese boys must be getting pretty desperate, because by your standards none of the girls my age will be marriage material. All those boys will have to learn how to iron because it's going to be a long lonely life for them!'

I figure I've gone a little over the top because even Mum gives me a warning look.

'They'll just go to Lebanon and marry a girl there,' Angela says, earning death stares from all three of us.

'Dad,' I say, sighing, 'I don't care about the neighbours, they're going to gossip anyway –'

'Yes, Sophie, they are. I would just rather they did not talk about us. I have had enough to deal with in this life.'

'Okay, Dad, next time I'm out at three in the morning, I'll call and ask you to come pick me up. And next time –'

'I am not finished, Sophie. What you did was wrong. And you won't be out at three in the morning *ever* if I have anything to do with it. These streets are no place for a girl like you. Or any girls. The world out there is dangerous, and not everyone understands the sanctity of the woman like we do. This is the end of the discussion. It is done, we are finished.'

Tears well in my eyes and I get up from the table. I stuff my lunch into my bag with as much attitude as I can muster, taking out my frustrations on it. Outside I wait for Dad to unlock the doors of his taxi so that I can get in and be driven to Leila's house in time for my 11 am shift.

In the past two days, I've managed to lose my best friend and even more of my right to enjoy my adolescence. I wonder what joys life has in store for me next.

12

I hate that there's no reliable map for finding my place in the world

I arrive at Leila's with red-rimmed eyes and the weight of the world on my shoulders. But she doesn't seem to notice and is strangely quiet on the drive to work.

'Soph, just a heads-up,' she says after a while. 'Next Friday night I'm not coming to dinner, and I won't be home Saturday either so I won't be able to hang out or do a sleepover.'

'Aww, that sucks,' I say. 'That'll make it two Fridays without me.'

She doesn't say anything. Her hands are gripping the steering wheel tight, as if she's holding the car together.

'Is there anything wrong? Anything I can help with?' I ask.

'Nope, sorry, kid,' she says, giving me a half-smile. 'Just some personal stuff.'

'Oh, okay,' I say quietly.

'Sorry, babe. I have a lot on at the moment.'

'Nothing I can help out with?' I ask again, hopefully.

'Nah, not really, just … something with Lisa.'

'Can't I stay at your house anyway?'

'Sophie, come on, it's just one time. You don't have to act like a child.'

'I'm not acting like a child. I would've liked a little more notice, that's all.'

'Well, I said I was sorry. Things come up at the last minute when you're an adult.'

I don't respond, but the scowl on my face says everything. The exchange when she drops me off at work is terse and I get out of the car in a hurry, my eyes brimming with tears again. The one person I thought I could rely on doesn't have time for me anymore.

I check my phone for a message from Dora before I put my bag into my locker. Nothing. Clearly she isn't interested in whether or not I got home safely. Big winner of a friendship there!

I pack stock in silence until it's time for my break. I'm thankful that I'm not on registers today – the interaction would kill me. I go to grab my bag from my locker and run into Casey in the staffroom.

'Hey, lady,' she says, smacking her locker door shut. 'Long time no see. Are you coming to my party or what?'

I shake my head. She looks disappointed and I feel ashamed, even though it isn't my fault.

'What could be more important than my coming of age?' she asks, cocking her head at me. 'A wedding with four hundred and fifty people? No one will miss you if there's that many, even if you're faaabulous.'

'It's complicated,' I say. And then I come out with it. 'My parents are really strict. Well, my dad is. He's extremely traditional, plus he worries *a lot*. I'm only allowed to go to functions if the person is from school or if my parents know the family. Not personally, necessarily, but like their village or something. Or if they're friends of friends or whatever.'

'A village?' she asks, looking at me curiously. 'Tell your dad he's in Australia now – we call them suburbs here. Anyway, it's no biggie. I understand.'

She starts to walk out then stops at the door. 'Sophie?'

'Yeah?'

'Try not to be too hard on them, okay? You're lucky that you have parents who really care about what you do and who you hang out with. Trust me on that.'

I give her a half-smile and watch her walk away, then make my own way outside via the shortcut. Shehadie is sitting on a bench near the bus stop outside the centre. He glances up from the book he's reading, then puts it down, watching me. I can tell from the look on his face that we're both in the same headspace at that moment. If we were at school I wouldn't even consider hanging out with him, but at work it's different. So I risk the irritation that his company will no doubt bring and walk over.

'I got in trouble from my dad,' I say, putting my bag down. I'm surprised by my honesty, but there's something about him that makes me feel really comfortable.

'I'm sorry, Soph. How come?'

I shrug. 'Because I got a lift from a guy.'

'I don't get it,' he says.

'I don't expect you to.'

'Are you gonna let me try? Who knows, it might be more interesting than the adventures of Tatiana and Alexander.' He nods towards his book.

'You're reading *The Bronze Horseman*?' I ask, shocked.

He laughs, a genuine, open laugh that lights up his face.

I find myself staring at him, surprised by my longing.

'Why are you so stunned?' he says.

'It's kind of a chick's book. No wonder you don't play footy with the boys at lunch.'

'A friend from my old school is making me read it. She's in love with the series. She read the first two in a week – the bags under her eyes were huge,' he says, laughing again. 'I quite like the historical stuff. It's set in World War II. Have you read it?'

'Yeah, my aunty recommended it to me. She loved the whole trilogy, but I've only read the first one. The sex scenes freaked me out a bit,' I say, then regret being so open. Heat flames my cheeks.

'Well, I *am* an eighteen-year-old boy,' he says, smiling knowingly.

I bite my lip awkwardly and look away.

'So, tell me why you're in trouble,' he says. 'You seem like you're carrying the world on your shoulders.'

'Long story,' I say, groaning and burying my head in my hands.

'I got time.'

'It's "I *have* time",' I point out.

'You're a know-it-all pain in the arse, Sophie. I don't know why I want to help you.'

He picks up his book and pretends to ignore me, dramatically turning his back to me, but then he glances over and smiles.

I smile too, but it's sad and pathetic. 'I can't win. And I'm tired of trying,' I say.

'Not a lot of information there, but I'll try to work with it,' he says. 'So, knowing your tendency for melodrama,

I have to ask, are you really trying to win whatever it is that needs winning?' He raises an eyebrow, waiting for my answer.

'I'm just over everything,' I say. 'The curfews, the rules, the drama, the difference between my brother and me – why he gets to have a life and I don't, just because I'm a girl.'

He's about to say something but I keep going.

'I'm over the people at school too. It's like they're content to live in a square and it irritates the hell out of me. It's like they have the smallest minds and they want to keep them that way. Do you know how much Vanessa and her friends make fun of me because my Society and Culture methodology is on asylum seekers? Or because I ask questions in class? Heaven forbid anyone might want to learn something at school as opposed to showcase her new lip gloss.'

He raises his arms in surrender. 'You're preaching to the converted here. Look at the guys at CSC. I made the rugby league team and I've played three matches already – you'd think they'd invite me to play at lunchtime with them, if only for the sake of improving our skills, but no. They'd rather lose to other schools than invite the Aussie to join in for a bit of extra practice.'

'Yeah, it's pretty bullshit,' I say. 'They're still so narrow-minded about you.'

'Life is bullshit,' he says, scuffing the ground with the toe of his big black boot. He's worn them to school a few times and the nuns have gone ballistic – they think they're too 'goth'. 'You can't let it get you down. And you have to remember that Vanessa and her friends aren't an accurate representation of people at our school. Just like ethnic gangs aren't an accurate representation of an entire cultural community. I think people let them get away with that crap because, like you, they don't want to deal with their narrow-mindedness.'

I nod, thinking it over.

'But can I ask,' he goes on, 'why the hell is your dad so old-fashioned? You'd think he'd have gotten over it by now.'

I sigh. 'I think part of it comes from living in the area we do. Having so many Lebanese around means that he doesn't have to mix with other people. The people he knows are all migrants like him, people who remember Lebanon like it was in the seventies. They don't get that Lebanon's moved with the times and is probably more modern now than a small town in the American Midwest. And he's especially strict with me because he doesn't want me getting caught up in a more Australianised world, where girls move out of home before they get married or spend the night at their boyfriend's house. It's not just about giving gossipers the ammo to talk, but about breaking certain traditions, like a girl only moving out of home on her wedding day. It's the reason why there's always a massive pre-wedding celebration in Lebanese families, to say farewell.'

'That's nice, though,' he says.

'Yeah, there are some really nice things about tradition. But they're not the things that get me down. I still want my culture and traditions to be part of my life – I'm not chucking that away. I just want them to be more realistic, more in keeping with the time and place we live in, more equal.'

'Which is where your brother comes in?' he asks.

'Exactly! He has different rules because he's male. Because he's the one who asks for a girl's hand in marriage, his prospects can't be ruined. A girl's reputation is a lot more fragile in our culture. According to my brother, my marriage prospects are hanging by a thread because I believe in equal rights and I'd expect my husband to help me around the house and stuff. Apparently, being feisty or feminist makes me too Australianised, which translates to rejecting the traditional Lebanese notion of marriage.'

'But you are Australian.'

'By birth, yes, but I still practise a lot of my Lebanese customs. Which means I don't just get hassled by Lebanese people unwilling to understand Australian values, but also by ignorant Australians. I hate that we get stereotyped so much as Lebanese people. We're either all in gangs, or we're drug dealers who shoot at each other in the street. They assume that we're all Muslim, and that all Muslim people must be terrorists. A few months ago, I was talking to an old lady and eating hot chips at the same time and she asked me why I wasn't fasting for Ramadan. Dora once overheard a boy telling his friend that their Greek classmate had converted to Lebanese, but what he was trying to say was that the guy had converted to Islam.'

Shehadie cracks up laughing.

'It's not funny!' I say, shoving him. 'We stereotype Aussies and they stereotype us, and that means there's never going to be any hope for either of us, because neither group really knows what the other group's about.'

'Yeah, but people aren't as racist as you think. I mean, they all care about boat people,' he points out.

I sigh. 'Shehadie, please tell me you're not that ignorant. It's all well and good to march through the streets calling for better treatment of refugees, but seriously, how many people even care what happens after the boat people have landed in Australia? They march, and then they go back to their comfortable lives in the eastern suburbs or the north shore or whatever. It's the rest of us who see the real face of migration, what happens when we just forget about the refugees. They move into the same areas, because of course that's where they feel comfortable, surrounded by their own people, but then the wider population starts to question why they don't work, or why they don't interact, or learn Australian values, or speak the language, or whatever else comes up in some "letters to the editor" section in a newspaper. People don't get that some of them really want to be here, to function in society, but there isn't enough support to help them set up their lives. We need more education and assimilation – not to the extent that migrants have to forget who they are, but enough to bring them into the wider community rather than living on the fringe.

'I mean, look at my parents. I love them to death, but I know my dad's a bit backward. His relatives in Lebanon have moved with the times – girls there are allowed to stay out past midnight without a chaperone, and date boys outside their village, and they don't have to go to every family function under the sun – but my dad refuses to accept that. He thinks his village is the exact same way it was when he left it. And the funny thing is, he's pretty tame compared to some other dads – he doesn't expect me to go to Lebanon at eighteen and marry my cousin.'

'I don't understand,' Shehadie says. 'My grandparents aren't like that.'

'They can't afford to be. Your mother marrying an Anglo forced them to wake up and look at things differently, even if it took them a long time. They saw a different way of living and realised that it was okay, it didn't ruin anything. Their relationship with their daughter wasn't jeopardised in the long run, her marriage lasted, and her son still knew where he came from. I mean, you're at a Leb school, for God's sake.'

'But whether I belong there is an entirely different matter,' he says. 'Do you really think there can be a middle ground?'

'There has to be,' I say. 'For my sake, at least. Because while I'm here in Australia, I'm always going to be an ethnic. And in Lebanon, I'll always be the *Australiyee*. So if there's no middle ground, then I don't belong anywhere.'

13

I hate that I've been stupid enough to buy into the 'friends forever' bullshit

By the time Sunday comes around, I've still had no word from Dora. Facebook is littered with photos from Friday night, and even though I spot myself in a few, looking like I'm having the time of my life, I log off and avoid it. I know how the night pans out: my years-long friendship with Dora dissolves because it can't withstand the pressures of high school.

I go to school on Monday with a gnawing pain in my gut. I know that things with Dora can't go back to normal, but I'm not prepared to face whatever happens next. A public fight? A fake friendship? Or an awkward search for new friends to help me see out the year?

I see Dora sitting with Vanessa's posse, giggling with Rita over God knows what, as I make my way through the quad. I don't call out to her, just smile at her from afar. She doesn't move, and Rita looks at me with disdain, like she feels sorry for me.

I guess Dora reconsiders, because she comes up to me as I'm walking towards my locker before the bell rings for assembly. 'Soph, can I talk to you for a sec?'

I shrug. 'Sure. Though I can't for the life of me think what about.'

'Now's not the time for your sarcasm,' she says, folding her arms. 'What happened on Friday was shit and I'm not going to deny it. But it made me realise that we're at two different points in our lives right now. I told you at the start of this year that I wanted something more. I want to enjoy being young while I can, and I thought you wanted the same thing. We're teenagers, we have to lie to our parents sometimes. You need to live a little.'

'Dora, let's forget about Dictator Dad for a second and think about it. This isn't just about me lying to my parents to live a little. I don't want to do that at the expense of my safety, driving around with a guy who's been boozing it up –'

'He didn't drink that much, I asked him,' she interjects. 'And he waited an hour or so before he started driving.'

'It doesn't matter – he's on his Ps, which means he's not allowed to drink at all. I don't care how big or hairy he is, he's still technically not a man yet. Plus, even if we forget about the drinking, you still did a pretty dodgy thing by not even calling to see if I got home okay. You didn't care about me even as an afterthought.'

'I know, I stuffed up,' she says, sighing. 'You know I love you, right, but I don't want to spend my last year in high school being a loser. I have fun with those girls.'

'You have fun with those girls because they get their high from thinking they're better than everyone else,' I say. 'And they treat everyone else that way. If that's what it means to be popular, then I'd rather be the biggest loser that ever lived. I want my friends to look at me and say, I'm glad I have you by my side because you'll never let me down, no matter what else is on offer. Rita doesn't fit into that category. So I guess you have to ask yourself if you're really willing to destroy a good friendship for someone who might not think you're worth it in a few weeks' time.'

I can see Rita watching us, and even though I sound tough I want to disappear into thin air. I don't want to give her the satisfaction of seeing me fight this out with Dora, especially as my eyes are about to flood the quad with tears.

'That's slack, Skaz,' Dora says, twirling a piece of her hair. 'And it's not even true. Trust me, if you get to know her, she's not like that.'

'I knew her way before you did. And she's always been the same — happy to let things slide when something better comes along. Come to think of it, maybe you guys are a perfect fit after all.'

She sighs. 'We can still hang out, you know. Nothing has to change — well, not everything, anyway.'

'Dora,' I say, exasperated, 'you left me alone in the city at night. I didn't even have a lift home. Good friends don't abandon each other like that, especially when they have no way of getting home. Six months ago you would've declared anyone who did that a bitch.'

I get a half-smile response; she knows I'm right. We used to laugh and joke around together. Now, there are only awkward silences and stupid explanations about what we feel and think and do. I want to walk away, but Dora is still standing there, caught between the old and familiar and the new and exciting. If I'm honest, I can't really blame her. I wish I was the type of person worth turning down the world's biggest party for.

'I guess I saw this coming,' I finally say. 'Friday just brought it on. You stopped calling, stopped waiting for me after homeroom. When you did call, it was only about homework.' She opens her mouth to say something but I'm on a roll. 'No more immediate responses on Facebook, no more after-school hangouts on Fridays, barely any text messages.'

'I don't know what to say to you, Soph.'

'Then don't say anything,' I reply, heaving my bag onto my shoulders. 'I'll be okay,' I tell her. 'Really, I will.'

The bell rings, and Dora rejoins Rita while I walk alone to the assembly hall wondering how I'm going to get through the next few months without a best friend.

—⁂—

I'm in a foul mood all through Economics and Business, then head straight for the staffroom when recess hits, hoping to catch Mrs Cafree so I can ask her a question about my methodology. When the bell rings for us to go back to class, I'm relieved to have survived my first break without any friends.

The next few lessons pass by in a blur thanks to the fact that I completely tune out, which earns me a lunchtime detention from my Maths teacher.

I walk into the detention room, kick my bag under my desk and lay my head on the table. At least I don't have to worry about who I'm going to hang out with over lunch. Perhaps I should aim to make this a regular thing? It'd even give me extra time to get my school work done. My brilliant plan is abandoned when Shehadie walks in and plonks himself into the seat next to me.

'What a waste of a lunchtime,' he says, rolling his eyes. 'What are you in here for?' He asks as if we're friends, in school anyway.

'I forgot my calculator and refused to share someone else's,' I say bluntly, because clearly we're not friends.

'That's all? Geez, this school's discipline policy is like pot luck.'

I laugh inwardly but make no effort to keep the conversation going. I have to hand it to him, though, he has persistence.

'So how are you feeling after the weekend?' he asks. 'Are you okay?'

I slide a look at him that says 'shut up', but he doesn't get it.

'I saw you talking to Dora this morning –'

'Shehadie,' I say, exasperated, 'I don't really want to talk today.'

'Okaaaay,' he replies, holding his hands up in front of his chest. 'I just think it'd be stupid of you to let it slide, you know.'

'Yes, because that's the core message at my Catholic school: don't let it slide. Don't turn the other cheek, forgive and forget, blah blah blah.'

'What she did was slack. Not that I want to get in the middle of your friendship or anything, but to me that's not really friendship so I'm just going to say it. You'd be an idiot if you forgot what she did.'

I glare at him.

'That's what I'd tell my sister, if I had one,' he adds. 'I'm sure your brother would say the same.'

'You don't know my brother,' I mutter, pulling my journal out of my bag. 'Now if you don't mind, I'm going to let it all out in my journal.'

He smirks at me. 'Girls with journals end up becoming cat ladies, you know.'

'Shehadie,' I snap. 'Shut up.'

And with that, the conversation is over.

Clearly, the boys have decided it's interfere-with-Sophie's-bad-mood day because Zayden sits next to me in fourth period. Under normal circumstances, this would have made me squeal with delight, but today my heart sinks when I realise he's just here to talk about Friday night.

'How are you going, Sophie?' he says with a smile.

'Okay,' I reply half-heartedly.

'Listen, Soph,' he continues, pulling his stuff out of his school bag and placing it on the desk. 'I just want to say no harm done, you know. Sometimes we get a bit carried away when we want to have fun. I wish you could have come with us, but I guess it wasn't going to work out with your curfew and all.'

I shrug.

'But you know, you really need to be careful who you're hanging out with, because you never know if they really understand you.'

My face reddens. *Act cool, Sophie Kazzi, act cool. Even if it's an entirely foreign concept to you.*

'I'm not following you,' I say.

'Well, you know how our community can get a bit talkative, right?' He looks at me like he's trying to sell me girl-scout cookies.

'That's an understatement if there ever was one.'

'Right. You know all about it. So you know reputation's a big thing, especially for a girl. And especially when she comes from such a great family and all.'

Because you visit our home regularly and know our family dynamics? I go to interrupt him, but he's still talking.

'And you know how we're all protective of each other because not everyone understands us or views things the way that we do. And because of –'

'Zayden,' I cut in, surprised at my rashness, 'whatever it is you're trying to tell me, just say it.'

He stares at me, open-mouthed. I guess he's surprised by my rashness too.

'I think you should be careful,' he says finally. 'Some people saw you going home with that Aussie boy.'

'He has a name,' I say, softly this time. 'And he's half-Lebanese – not that it should matter what he is.'

He scoffs. 'It's not like we can see any Lebanese side. Anyway, it looks bad. Girls like you shouldn't be out with guys like him.'

'Girls like me? Zayden, you don't even know me. Why are you suddenly so concerned? You've never really spoken to me before. Why now? Why this guy?'

I find his blatant racism disturbing. Even more so than the fact he thinks I'd do what he says, just because that's what he's used to. I want to ask him how he plans to function in the world outside of high school. But I don't. I'm not sure that concept has even occurred to him yet.

'They want us out of the country, Sophie. The least we can do is keep them out of our lives.'

'Come on, Zayden, they don't want us out of the country. The governor of New South Wales is a Lebanese *woman*, for heaven's sake. Her husband captained the Wallabies. And the former premier in Victoria was a Lebanese man.'

He stares at me blankly and opens his mouth to say something, but I beat him to it.

'You can't take that one stupid comment that led to the Brighton Brawl seriously. We don't even know what it was – it's all Chinese whispers!'

'So you start getting cosy with that Aussie guy and suddenly you no longer have any loyalty to who you are? What about my little cousin, Soph?'

'Zayden, I swear to you, I think it's terrible George got hurt. I was distraught for him and his family. But not every Aussie person thinks like that, and not every Aussie person deserves to be treated the way you're treating Shehadie. I mean, how would you like it if every Aussie started treating us like we all condone gang rape just because of the actions of a few animals?'

'So you're not going to stop talking to him? For your own good?'

'Is this what it comes down to? The guy's not even my friend, Zayden. I just think it wouldn't kill any of us to show him some courtesy. Lebanese people are supposed to be among the most generous on the planet. Are you trying to tell me that if an Aussie guy walked into your home, your parents wouldn't welcome him with open arms? Give him the meal of his life and five-star hotel treatment? That's about honouring our culture too ... and Shehadie is a visitor to this school, after all. What's more, he's just a kid like you and me.'

'I thought you were smarter than that, Sophie. You're better off sticking with your own kind. I'm not saying that non-Lebanese aren't good people, I'm just saying that we do things differently. We think differently, we act differently.

Plus, imagine how your dad would react to you being friends with an Aussie guy. Your brother even.'

There's truth in what he's saying about my dad and brother, even if I don't want to admit it. Maybe that was one of the reasons Leila hadn't ended up marrying Peter. I realised I'd never even asked her what happened on that front.

'We're not going out or anything,' I say. 'We don't even like each other half the time. You know me – I talk to everyone. I like to give people a chance.'

By now, the class has settled down and our teacher is starting the lesson.

'That's nice,' Zayden whispers, opening up his textbook. 'But not everyone deserves a chance. Especially when they don't dish them out themselves.'

'If you follow that philosophy,' I whisper back, 'then you're saying it's okay for society to judge us based on what they see about Lebanese gangs in the newspapers. But not everyone thinks that way, and Shehadie's one of those people who's smart enough to know better, no matter where he grew up.'

Zayden looks at me for a second and shrugs. 'We all have to suffer stereotypes in our lifetime. And not all of us can do anything about it.'

Can't or won't, I wonder. I think about the fact that lots of the people around me are content to live in their little squares, without ever considering the plights of others. Suddenly the phrase 'ignorance is bliss' makes perfect sense, and I understand why half the kids at my school have pretty blissful lives.

Tuesday. Another Dora-less school day. I spend recess in the library borrowing books for my Business Studies assignment, but still obsessing about how my friendship with Dora has got to this point. Then again, if the articles in *Girlfriend* have taught me anything, it's that to some people popularity is everything. Sad thing is, I hadn't realised Dora was 'some people'.

At lunchtime, I see her. I'm walking down the stairs that face the seniors' area of the quad when I suddenly feel self-conscious, aware that Rita, Vanessa and Dora are hanging out on a bench a few metres in front of me. Besides a small nod in my direction, Dora doesn't acknowledge me. If they didn't already, the whole school now knows that our friendship is officially over.

The backpack on my shoulders seems heavier than usual, the stairs longer, the quad a hell of a lot bigger. I think about how I preferred it when Vanessa and Co. didn't know I existed. Instead, I'd come so close to being one of them and then got screwed over at the last minute because I couldn't shake my ability to listen to my gut. It might be a good thing in an adult, but for a seventeen-year-old, it's a curse.

Across the quad, Shehadie is reading a book under the pergola, like he's done every day since he came to CSC. Zayden and a few other boys from our class are playing football, and as usual they don't ask him to join in. Instead, they ignore him, or occasionally throw a snide remark his way. My eyes meet Shehadie's and he smiles. I smile back awkwardly, and look from him to Vanessa's group, like we're all part of some confusing game.

I start to walk over to him, but my fear gets the better of me and I go into the toilets instead. I sit in a cubicle, take out my journal and doodle over some of the pages.

After five minutes, I'm over being so pathetic and make my way to the library. Mrs Morton, the librarian, sings out my name as I walk in.

'Back again today?' she says.

I nod, embarrassed.

'Don't worry, we'd rather thirty of you than half the other kids in here.' She gestures to the noisy juniors milling about. 'Plus, I bet we're good for you too. You must be making headway on all your assessments.'

'Something like that,' I say. 'Got anything new for me?'

'Actually, I ordered something that I think you'll really love,' she says. 'If you man the sign-in book for a moment, I'll go find it. Ms Richards is at the canteen stocking up on chocolate for her 2 pm craving so I'm on my own right now.'

She returns holding a novel for me and my face lights up. There are definite perks to having a good relationship with the librarian.

'Diane Armstrong's *Empire Day*,' she says. 'As soon as I read the blurb I knew it would be perfect for you. It's set in Sydney in 1948 and looks at some of the issues around post-war migration. It'll be useful for your Society and Culture assessment, but I thought the themes – identity, ethnicity, belonging – would interest you anyway.'

'Wow, Mrs Morton, am I that transparent?'

She smiles. 'Let's just say your borrowing record says a lot about your interests. Now, it's not officially on the system yet, so please take care of it and bring it back as soon as you're done.'

'I always do,' I say, grinning. 'Thanks heaps. I appreciate it.'

And just like that, I have even more of an excuse to spend the rest of the week in the library. Books, unlike people, never let me down.

14

I hate feeling like I don't have a say in my own life

My parents have a barbecue for Mother's Day and invite our entire extended family. With eleven adults and fifteen kids, the lunch is pretty much chaos, and as usual the women do all the work. Not a very good Mother's Day present if you ask me, but no one ever does.

The men sit like kings at the table, talking Lebanese politics and drinking beer, while their wives hover in the kitchen and carry out plates of food. Clearly this level of service isn't enough, because intermittently my dad or uncle asks one of us girls to go fetch something else for them, like another drink or some garlic sauce or more bread.

I sit at the edge of a long table, which is actually four tables joined together and covered by one of those plastic tablecloths you get at a two-dollar store, astounded at the patriarchal crap that makes my family go round.

Eventually, the topic of conversation turns to me. '*Khabrina ya*, Sophie,' my uncle's wife, Paula, says to me. 'What are you going to do next year? University, *mesh hayk*?'

It's a rhetorical question, because to them uni is the only option. It figures, given ninety per cent of our family are migrants whose sole purpose for coming here was to give their kids an education.

Dad responds on my behalf before I have a chance to speak.

'She's going to apply for business and commerce and come out of uni an accountant,' he says, smiling. 'She does so well at Business Studies at school, and Economics and even Mathematics.'

Everyone at the table murmurs their approval, except Leila, who shakes her head. No one notices except me.

'We couldn't keep her in the Two-unit Extension Maths,' Dad goes on. 'But General Maths is all she needs if she wants to do accounting. They have a bridging course at the University of Western Sydney – close to home in Milperra. She needn't give her father a big heart attack by being too far away.'

'Allah amir hal balad,' my uncle says, pleading with God to continue to build up his adopted homeland. 'There are universities everywhere. And they even give the students financial assistance to study. Not like in the old country, eh?'

Dad nods, even though he rarely steps outside of his little Lebanese enclave.

'Sophie will do well no matter what she does,' Paula says, smiling. 'She's a very good girl.'

'Yes, she is,' Dad says proudly, pleased at the comment. 'She listens to her father, respects her mother, does what she is meant to do.'

Later, when Leila and I are drying the dishes, she asks me how I feel about going to uni.

'I'm not sure,' I tell her. 'But I know I don't want to do accounting or business. I'd love to do something with a bit more passion behind it.'

'You can't fight for something if you don't know what it is, Soph. What do you like to do?'

I shrug. 'I don't know, I guess something creative maybe, like drama or photography or interior design. Or even art.'

She looks at me, bemused. 'You doing art? Remember that Van Gogh piece you had to copy in Year Seven? What a disaster you made of a great painting!'

I laugh and shove her. 'Don't be mean. I know I can't draw, but I like art. I could study all the great artists and interpretations of their work, and I could run a gallery.'

'Let's be realistic rather than whimsical,' she says. 'What can you actually see yourself doing? You have a lot of opinions, and when you're feeling confident you usually argue them well. Plus, you're interested in social issues. You could become one of those pro-bono lawyers?'

I make a face. 'I just want to do something I really believe in and feel passionate about,' I explain. 'There's no passion in accounting ... or in numbers.'

'Unless it's the numbers you rack up on your credit card after a splurge at Cosmopolitan Shoes!'

Leila and I both laugh, and then she turns away to wipe the benchtops. She looks tired, and I remember how she was stressed last time I'd seen her.

'Are you okay, Leila?' I ask. 'You don't seem like your usual self.'

'Just a lot happening at work, kid,' she replies, but I know she's lying. She's usually pretty blasé about work, so I don't understand why she's fobbing me off.

'I gotta go to the bathroom,' she says awkwardly. 'You should go study a bit. Heaven forbid you don't get into that accounting course at the uni that's ten minutes away ...' She makes a face at me and leaves the room.

I do head up to my room to do some work, but I'm too distracted. I hop online and browse through some uni websites. Now that I think about it, I really want to go to a city university. I browse through the programs at Notre Dame, UTS and Sydney Uni, hoping to find a course that speaks to me.

A while later, I'm interrupted by the sound of Dad arguing with someone. I look out the window and notice that my relatives' cars are no longer there. Only Leila's remains. I tiptoe out of my room, careful not to make any noise, and hide on the landing upstairs.

'You don't know if it's really the case. Why would you open up old wounds?' Dad says.

'Old wounds for you or old wounds for me, Elias?' Leila sounds exasperated. 'What the hell is the matter with you?'

'Nothing would be the matter with me if you did the right thing!' he bellows. 'But you never change! You are always causing dramas and dilemmas for this family. Why can't you ever make a choice that is suitable?'

'Because no choice is suitable unless it is *your* choice,' Leila says slowly. 'Your daughter's a grown woman and you're still making choices for her and keeping her trapped. But she's living under your roof and you are her father, so even though I want to, I won't interfere. But, mark my words, it will come back to bite you.'

'Don't talk to me like that,' he snaps.

'I can say whatever I want, because you can't control me,' Leila retorts. 'You never have and you never will. I'm leaving. Please thank Theresa for lunch.'

I step back quickly so she can't see me as she walks down the hall and slams the front door behind her.

—∿—

Dad's in a bad mood for the rest of the afternoon, and dinner is uncomfortably quiet. Afterwards, I follow Andrew into his room to ask him if he heard anything.

'Why are you being nosey?' he demands. 'If people are having problems, they don't need you poking yourself into their business.'

I think back to the days when I had a good relationship with my brother. Now he seems to think that 'becoming a man' gives him licence to be an asshole.

'Hey, relax,' I say. 'I just wanted to know if they were okay. It sounded bad.' I turn to walk out the door.

'Yeah, and it'll probably get worse if you interfere in something that has nothing to do with you,' he says. 'And that goes for being friends with that Shire boy too.'

I spin around. 'How do you know about that?'

'I have my sources,' he says, getting off the bed to switch on the Wii and grab his joystick. 'It's not making you look good, sis. So you better stop now before we all start suffering from your bad reputation.'

'Now look who's interfering,' I argue. 'What's any of that got to do with you? First of all, the guy's half-Lebanese and has just as much right to go to our school as you and me. And everyone who treats him like crap isn't behaving very

Christian, if you ask me. Isn't that more important to the school than cultural loyalty?'

'Don't pretend you know anything about loyalty to our culture,' he says. 'Now get out. I have to play a bit before I go to bed, otherwise I can't relax.'

Back in my room, I flop on the bed and stare at the ceiling. What the hell is going on with everyone?

Grabbing my phone out of my back pocket, I send an SMS to Leila.

> Hey, I want 2 come hang out this wk after work. Sat &
> Sun, totes need a break from Dad. OK by u?

Two hours later, by the time I go to bed, I still don't have a response.

—◦◦◦—

> Sorry sweets, real busy ATM, but we'll catch up
> soon, I swear. Sure mum or dad can take u to work in
> meantime. Just have a lot goin on xx

Leila's reply, a day later, buckles me. She's never this distant. I wonder what's happened, but I know I'm not going to get the answers from Mum or Dad. I think about it the entire week, moping around because I've never felt so alone before, especially now I don't even have Dora.

At work, Casey corners me in the staffroom about her birthday. 'So you've officially declined my invitation?' she asks.

'Yeah, sorry about that. It was never going to happen for me.'

'It's okay, I understand,' she says, shrugging. 'Although I'd much prefer you were coming than some other people.' She eyes Morgan, who's getting up from the lunch table.

'Am I missing something?' I say. 'You invited Morgan?'

She makes a face. 'Well, he sort of invited himself.'

'He's like twenty-eight! How are you even friends?'

'I'm embarrassed to tell you,' she says. 'We hooked up once – at the Christmas party last year. No one knows. If they did, I'd never live it down.'

My eyes widen.

'Don't ever get drunk at work functions, because you'll never end up with someone cute, like Shehadie or Jordan or even Hayden Williams,' she adds. 'It's always the losers who're available.'

'Um, all I can say is *eww*. What were you thinking? He's not even your type! You wear sparkly tutus and do ballet. He listens to Iron Maiden and dyes his hair black and has ugly tattoos.'

'I *wasn't* thinking!' she hisses. 'I was drunk! Come on, as if you've never hooked up with anyone regrettable?'

I shake my head.

'No one?' she says. 'As if.'

I redden. 'I haven't hooked up with anyone *full stop*,' I whisper.

It takes her a moment to register. 'So wait … you're a virgin?'

I nod.

'Oh, that is so old school. And cute.'

I make a face at her.

She shrugs. 'It's just a little surprising, that's all. It's not like you're unattractive. What are you waiting for?'

'What, so unattractive people don't have sex?' I ask, mocking her. 'It's not about that. I've decided to wait until I get married. No big deal.'

'No big deal? Are you for real?' She looks amused.

'Look, no judgement on anyone else,' I explain. 'It's just not for me. I'm not a prude. I just like to think of how much I'm sharing and who I'm sharing it with. I don't even wear really skimpy clothes. I like the idea of part of me remaining hidden.'

'Romance and mystery and all that?' she says.

'You're making fun of me,' I say, shoving her. 'But I want my husband to earn the right to my body. People complain that chivalry is dead, and some women might say that I'm not empowered. But I *feel* empowered by my choice; it makes me feel strong and in control. I think of feminism as going against the grain of what society expects, and in this day and age, sex is everywhere. So I want to be different. My body is sacred, so I want a guy to see me for my true worth first, and sometimes that takes a big commitment. Like marriage. It's not for everyone, but it's right for me.'

'Don't you worry about a guy not sticking around because of it?' she asks.

'Hell no, it's a great way of weeding out the bad ones,' I say, smiling. 'Not that I really know yet, but I guess I'd be upfront about it.'

'Wow.' She gives a long, low whistle that makes me laugh. 'You learn something new every day, don't you? It's not for me, but hey, kudos to you.'

She heads towards the door, then turns around. 'Hey, Sophie? That stuff you said about your body was nice. Maybe if we all thought like that, we'd have more self-esteem and fewer body issues.'

'That's a whole other kettle of fish,' I say. 'But either way, I'd appreciate it if you kept this conversation between us.'

'No problems,' she replies, walking out.

15

I hate it when the right thing is right in front of my face

A week goes by and I'm still stressing about Leila. On Tuesday at lunch, I'm writing in my journal in one of the library study rooms when two girls from my Society and Culture class, Sue Danneya and Nicole Nader, walk in.

'Oh, sorry, Sophie,' Sue says. 'Do you mind if we sit here for ten minutes? It's really noisy out there and I need to explain Nicole's Maths homework to her.'

'No problem,' I say. 'I'm not really writing anything important anyway. I think I'm bored and hungry.'

'Bored, I get,' Sue says. 'But how does a Lebanese person ever get hungry the way our mums stuff our lunch boxes?'

'I forgot mine,' I say. 'Mum can't have noticed otherwise she'd have brought it over.'

'Can I lend you some cash?' she asks.

'Oh no, it's all good, thanks. I already bought something from the canteen. It was gross though.'

She quickly explains an equation formula to Nicole, then plucks a mirror out of her bag and peers into it. 'Man, I can't stand these curls anymore. Just a bit of humidity and

I transform into a mad scientist. I swear Mr Bierden was laughing at me in Chemistry.'

'I think he was laughing about all the recognition he's gonna get when his mad scientist student gets the highest grade in the state for HSC Chemistry,' Nicole says.

'Thanks for the moral support. I'll be sure to put a "Don't let Nicole borrow" post-it on my ghd when it comes next week.'

'Ooooh, your mum finally bought it for you! Did I tell you how beautiful you look today?'

Sue laughs. 'Hurry up and do your Maths, we're gonna be late for choir.' She smiles at me apologetically. 'Sorry, Sophie, we're making it hard for you to concentrate.'

'Don't be silly,' I say. 'So you've got choir practice?'

'Yeah, once a fortnight. You should come with us if you're bored.'

I make a face.

'But you know, you don't have to,' she says when she sees my reaction.

'Nah, it's not that. I just can't sing.'

Sue grins. 'Actually, you'd be surprised at how much fun you'll have. Don't worry about the actual singing, sometimes we just hum in the background. There's a Year Nine student and two Year Ten girls who have amazing voices so we're usually just their background support.'

'Um, okay, why not?' I say. 'Got nothing better to do.'

'Woohoo, recruitment!' Nicole says, closing her textbook.

Sue gives her a death stare.

'What? I finished it, and did another equation too – just in case. Thanks for explaining it to me, my smart little cookie!'

'Nicole's had far too many sherbet sticks today,' Sue says.

'Actually, no, this behaviour's kind of normal. Using sugar as an excuse is a downright lie.'

I laugh.

We drop our bags off at the entrance to the seniors' building, then start walking to the church.

'So, how come you're not with Dora?' Nicole asks after a few minutes. 'Did you have a falling out or something? She's been spending a lot of time with Vanessa and that group lately, but I didn't even think they were friends.'

'Nicole, you idiot, that's none of your business,' Sue says, mouthing 'sorry' to me.

'Nah, it's okay,' I say. 'We're just into different things now, you know.'

'I don't mean to be nosey, but is that why you've been hanging out in the library?' Sue asks.

'You know what, I'm glad you came straight out and asked me to my face,' I say. 'I hate to think what people are saying behind my back.'

'To be honest, I think everyone knows what those girls are like,' Sue says, 'so everyone's probably glad for you.'

'Really?' I say. 'I've been feeling completely bummed about it. It's hard making new friends so late in high school. I can't really go up to groups and say, "Hey, can I be your friend?" when we've hardly spoken.'

'I don't think it'd be like that,' Sue says. 'I mean, I don't talk to everyone all the time, but we're all pretty friendly with each other. I doubt many people – unless they're precious – would turn you away. We're living in the age of social media – just because people don't sit together doesn't mean they're not interested in each other's lives.'

'Good point,' I say.

'Anyway, you're more than welcome to hang out with us,' she says. 'We're a mash-up of people. I'm the nerd, Nicole's the crazy, and Thomas and Jacob – well, they're a breed of their own.'

I smile.

'Speaking of the boys,' Nicole says, 'let's go find them.'

When the three of us join up with Thomas Aziz and Jacob Dib, I'm surprised that they don't even question my presence. Then again, maybe it is only the likes of Zayden, Vanessa and their cliques who think they're superior to everyone else.

'Guess what, boys?' Nicole announces, spreading her arms as if she's about to use them as wings, 'We have a new addition to our group. Sarcastic Sophie has joined us!'

'How do you know I'm sarcastic?' I ask. 'We haven't hung out together since some random activity at Year Ten camp!'

Sue laughs. 'In high school, everyone thinks nobody else notices them. They've got no idea how many people are watching, but choosing not to say anything because it's easier that way.'

I walk into the church after them and genuflect. Thank you, God, I sigh, smiling for real for the first time in weeks. Today, I feel like there is nothing invisible about me, and *that* feels so damn good.

—⁂—

On Thursday, Sister Magdalena calls a seniors' assembly first thing in the morning. It means we miss out on a class, so everyone's excited and curious about the reason.

'Seniors, earlier this year a police officer came to our school as part of an initial investigation into the Brighton Brawl and the associated retaliation that saw tens of thousands of dollars in property damage,' Sister Magdalena says, surveying the room. 'At that stage, the police were still piecing the puzzle together. Now they believe they have some leads that many of you may be able to help with.'

We're all hanging on her every word, as if we're in a movie theatre, waiting for a revelation.

'I will meet with the officers first to see what they need to do, and we'll discuss possible candidates for them to interview.'

People start whispering. Zayden and his friends look worried, while Vanessa and her friends are intrigued. I scan the group for Shehadie – he's reading a book hidden in his lap, glancing up occasionally and pretending to listen. He catches my eye for a second and smiles, but I look away.

'The police will need parental permission for the interviews, so I will be calling the parents of those students affected,' Sister Magdalena continues. 'Just in case you lot decide to lose the permission slip or forge a signature, I urge you to please remember that the police are on the side of justice and it's our duty to help them in any way we can.'

She finishes off with a prayer and sends us back to class, but all day it's the only thing anyone talks about.

At lunch, I meet up with Sue, Nicole, Jacob and Thomas, who are still debating whether or not it's a good idea to let the police interview students.

'No way!' Thomas says. 'It's a terrible idea.'

'And why's that?' Sue snaps. 'Do you think the people who did it should go unpunished? They did something stupid and they deserve to cop the flak for it.'

'We're totally with you on the copping-the-flak part,' Jacob says. 'But why bring it into school grounds? Zayden's on fire. No one wants to get burnt, but if they talk to the police, that's what'll happen.'

'I don't understand why he cares so much,' Sue says. 'Like, he must *really* love his cousin to be this protective of him over what happened.'

'I reckon it also comes back to proving a point to Shehadie,' I say. 'Zayden wants to be the big winner in the invisible contest those two are having.'

'Well, I say bring it on if it makes things a little more dramatic around here,' Nicole says, her eyes sparkling. 'I've been so bored lately. When did we all get so boring?'

'Nicole, just do your homework and get on top of the HSC and worry about the excitement part later,' Sue says. 'Okay, sweetie?'

'You need to stop mothering her,' Jacob says. 'She's going to be stuffed when you go your separate ways at uni.'

'Don't you worry, Jacob,' Nicole says. 'I plan on following her. All the way to the US if I have to.'

'Fiiiiiiigggggghhhhhttttt!'

The word echoes through the quad. We all look at each other, then get up and run towards the commotion.

'Oh my God,' Sue yells. 'Zayden and Shehadie are having a punch-up!'

'Are they serious?' I say. 'What the hell is wrong with them?'

We ask a Year Eleven girl nearby how the fight started.

'I dunno,' she says. 'I just saw the Aussie guy sitting there talking to that Abboud guy, then Zayden came up with two of his friends. He said something, and the Aussie guy didn't like it so he stood up in Zayden's face. Zayden said something else, and the Aussie guy just stood there with this smart-arse smirk on his face. Of course that made Zayden mad and he threw a punch.'

'So where's Abboud Guy now?' Thomas asked.

I give him a look and he rolls his eyes.

'Daniel Abboud, where is he?'

'He went to get the teachers and never came back,' the girl says.

'Typical,' Jacob says. 'That guy spends all his time playing video games with people fighting to the death, but in real life he's as useless as my grandma.'

By now, Zayden's buddies have broken up the fight, and Shehadie and Zayden are standing opposite each other with a crowd around them.

'You're just a piece of Anglo scum!' Zayden calls out. 'You lot reckon we've ruined your country? You ain't seen nothing yet if you want to rile us up.'

Shehadie just laughs at him. 'Dude, I don't even know why you're so riled up. You're seventeen – life's not that bad, get over it. So an Aussie guy came to your school? Boo hoo, deal with it. There are bigger problems in the world.'

'You don't belong here,' Zayden yells. 'I don't care what your name is. I don't care that your mum's dead or your dad abandoned you. Nobody wants you here.'

'Oh, shut up, Malouf,' Sue says. Zayden glares at her.

Shehadie shakes his head, then picks up his bag and starts to walk away.

'Don't listen to him, man,' Thomas says to him.

Jacob pats Shehadie on the back, along with a bunch of other people, but he keeps moving through the crowd, tossing his bag over the school fence and climbing over after it.

Just before he leaves, he turns and stares at me, a look of pure disappointment on his face. I stand there, rooted to the spot, my eyes not moving from the fence.

Mrs Cafree reaches the edge of the crowd. 'What's going on here?' she calls out.

As if on cue, everyone starts dispersing.

The Year Eleven girl seems disappointed that the drama is over. As she turns to go, Sue taps her on the shoulder.

'Yeah?' the girl asks.

'His name is Shehadie,' Sue says. 'Not "the Aussie guy". Shehadie. Same as your surname, right?'

She quickly walks off, embarrassed.

'I could kiss you right now,' I say to Sue, smiling.

'Ooooh, please don't,' she says. 'You're not my type at all.'

———⟋⟍———

'I heard there was a fight at school today,' Mum says at dinner that night.

Luckily, Dictator Dad is doing an extra taxi shift, so he isn't here to suggest I should stop going to school in case I get injured there as well.

'How do you know?' Andrew asks.

'How do you think?' Angela says. 'Lebanese-mum gossip.' She winks at Mum.

'One day it will be all yours, my darling,' Mum says.

Angela makes a face and covers her ears. 'And this will be my response to it!'

'Good girl,' Mum says. 'Life is better without it. It makes you think too much.'

'TV makes me think a lot,' Marie says. 'I want to know how people can film all those scary wild animals in the jungle. Or how they make movies under the sea. Sophie says I'm not allowed to put a camera in the water because it will wreck it.'

We all look at her puzzled little face and smile. And just like that, the conversation about the fight is over.

Later, Andrew comes into my room.

'If you get called by Sister Magdalena to talk to the cops, don't do it,' he says. 'All the boys are talking about how you're friends with that Aussie guy. I don't need cop stuff on top.'

I smirk. 'All the boys? Really? Geez, I've never been so popular.'

'Sophie!' he says, frustrated. 'I mean it.'

'Andrew, I'm not going to lie to the police. Since when did you get so cosy with Zayden and his friends, anyway?'

'You didn't see George that day,' he argues.

'Neither did you! It was New Year's Day, remember? We had everyone over.'

He seems startled. 'Whatever. I saw him later and he looked bad. Those people deserved what they got.'

I roll my eyes. 'The people who started it maybe. If we're stretching it. But the rest of the street? No way. I'm not lying to the cops, end of story.'

'Are you even listening to me?' he says. 'I don't want any more trouble at school. I'm in Year Ten, so for two and a half years I'll be known as the guy with that snitchy sister. Just listen to me and don't interfere in something that's got nothing to do with you.'

'What's any of this got to do with you?' I ask. 'So what if I help the police? I'm sick of seeing "Lebanese crime" every time I open the newspaper. The rest of us need to stand up and show that we don't condone the crimes of the minority.'

He looks at me disapprovingly. 'When did you get so high and mighty?' he says, slamming the door as he leaves.

I give Leila a call to tell her about the fight at school.

'Hi, sweetie,' she says. 'How's work? How's school? How are your new friends?'

'Everything's good. What about with you?'

'Things are okay. I'm busy doing a few —'

The call-waiting signal cuts her off.

'Oh, sorry, Soph,' she says. 'I need to take it. I'm sorry, I'll call you back as soon as I can.'

An hour later, still no phone call. I go to bed once again feeling like I don't matter.

16

I hate it when people can see right through me

The next Thursday, I dawdle out of homeroom and wander over to my locker to tidy it. I walk super slow, waiting for the corridor to clear so I'll have enough space to spread all my crap on the floor. Mum picked up my sisters earlier, after their sports carnival, so I have a lot of time. More importantly, she's given me rare permission to walk home.

I start pulling things out of my locker when I sense someone behind me – and it isn't the singing cleaner with his backpack-style vacuum and unwelcome comments about the youth of today. When I turn around, Shehadie is standing there, bag on one shoulder, his usual look of nonchalance on his face.

'Hi, Shehadie,' I say.

'Hey,' he says. 'What are you up to?'

'Ahh, you know, decluttering.' I'm holding a Maths test and an Economics assessment – both from Year Eleven. 'Maybe if I sort out the physical mess in my life, all the other messes will follow suit.'

'Is there anything you don't like to complain about?' he asks.

I tilt my head, close one eye and make out like I'm deep in thought. 'Hmmm, no. A big fat N-O spells no.'

'Righto,' he says, laughing. 'I'll keep that in mind.'

'So what's up?' I ask.

'Well, I was wondering where you've been for the past few days. I feel like I haven't seen you in ages.'

'I've been hanging around with Sue and Nicole's group at lunch, and they sit down near the front office. And, you know,' I shrug, 'I've just been busy with everything. So many assignments, so many dramas, so little Sophie time.'

'Fair enough,' he says, but I can tell he doesn't believe me. 'It's just that I couldn't help noticing that you've been a little distant with me.'

'Distant? How do you mean?'

'Really, Soph?' he says. 'There's no other way of saying it – it's like you're avoiding me. And I want to know why, because frankly I don't think I've done anything wrong.'

He rubs the back of his neck and I try not to notice how hot he looks. But I really can't handle this conversation right now.

'I swear, it's not you,' I say. 'You didn't do anything wrong.'

I shut my locker, pick up my bag and start walking. He falls in alongside me. I can't look at him.

'So why are you being so distant?' he says. 'On Tuesday, I could've sworn that you did a complete turnaround to avoid running into me in the corridor. And last week – I can't remember what day – you were coming down the stairs at lunchtime, saw me and ran.'

'I did kind of run, I guess, but I'd just remembered I had to do something for Maths –'

'The truth, Sophie.' He stops and catches my arm.

'It's just easier this way,' I say.

'What do you mean, easier?'

'Just simpler, like not having to explain anything to anyone.'

'So easier for other people, you mean? Like Zayden? And other idiots who shouldn't matter?'

I wonder if my brother is an idiot who shouldn't matter. The brother I used to be so close to, so protective of. The one who's in every childhood picture with me, holding my hand, riding a tricycle next to me, looking to me for approval. Where has my relationship with him gone? Has it become a casualty of Dad's attitude towards men and women? Or a casualty of our own differing views?

'It's not like that,' I protest, realising Shehadie is still waiting for a response. 'I just don't want things to be awkward. You know how it is here.' I scuff my foot on the floor. 'And things are already pretty hard at school as it is.'

'Things are hard for you, are they? Really? Do you get abused at school because of your surname? Or get punches thrown at you?'

I shake my head, feeling ashamed.

'Your friends came to my defence, but you didn't,' he goes on. 'Not that I needed anyone's help – it was just nice to know that someone was willing to speak out.'

'It's complicated,' I say. 'I already have a shitty reputation, I've lost my best friend and everything I do makes my brother mad. Suddenly, he's friends with Zayden and that lot. And you know how people here see you … I didn't want to make it worse. Plus –'

'I know damn well what people at this school think of me, Sophie,' he says quietly. 'I just didn't think that you were one of them.'

And then he walks away, leaving me even more confused about my role in this whole mess.

—⁂—

If there's one thing in the world worse than a Monday morning, it's a Monday morning that involves standing up in front of the class and making a fool of myself. And that's exactly what I'm faced with when I get to school and Sue reminds me we're being graded on a debate in Society and Culture. I hate public speaking more than school excursion bus rides, socks worn with sandals, and athletics carnivals combined, and my stomach starts churning as I walk along the corridor to class.

As soon as I see the topic written in huge underlined letters across the whiteboard, I know my dread was underrated.

Cedar Saints College should open its doors to students of other cultural backgrounds.

'Oh, brother,' Jacob says behind me. 'I can't deal with this kind of shit right now.'

'What do you mean?' Nicole says, nudging him. 'Society and Culture has never been so exciting.'

'Nicole, your optimism is really unnerving,' I snap.

Shehadie walks in and stops just inside the door. 'Oh, for the love of God,' he mutters. 'Can't a guy get a break around here?'

'Evidently not,' Jacob replies.

The two of them make their way to the back of the room, just as Mrs Cafree rises from her seat at the front.

'Settle down, please,' she calls out, before leading us in a prayer. Afterwards, she motions for us to sit down. 'Most of you have been at this school since you were infants. You've grown up with the people around you, you've formed different friendships over the years and you've become something like a family in the process.'

Someone grunts in the front row and she pauses to eyeball them.

'The other teachers and I have often wondered how you'll all fare in the big wide world when you leave CSC. Not because we doubt your abilities or social skills, but because we're concerned that you have a limited understanding of what goes on beyond these walls. It's going to be a massive adjustment when you realise you can't inject Arabic words into English sentences with everyone you meet, or when you discover that not everyone comes from the same style of family as you do. Not everyone you meet will be a church-goer and, sadly, not everyone is going to be accepting of you in the way they are here. Which is why I've chosen this particular topic for our debate over the coming week. No doubt many of you will respond with a no, but in the interests of strengthening your reasoning skills ahead of your HSC, you're going to have to present either the affirmative or negative side to the topic.'

Everyone starts whispering.

'It will be my decision which side you'll be on,' Mrs Cafree continues. 'I'm going to go around the room and give you a number. One is affirmative, two is negative. Once you have your number, the affirmatives move to the right side of the classroom and the negatives to the left. Each side is to nominate four speakers who will each have two minutes to present your arguments in the debate.'

I glance around the room. Zayden looks like he's just won the lottery. He turns around to tease Vanessa, who's sitting behind him, then catches sight of the miserable expression on Shehadie's face. He sneers at Shehadie, then raises his hand in the air.

'Yes, Zayden?' Mrs Cafree says.

'Miss, I think this an awesome topic –'

'Thank you.'

'– but I don't think it's going to make a difference to our attitudes.'

The class goes silent.

'I mean, it's nice what you're thinking and all that,' Zayden goes on, 'but nothing in life is fair. Certainly not for us, anyway.'

'Have you ever heard of the term "carrying your cross", Mr Malouf?' Mrs Cafree asks. 'Nothing in life is supposed to be fair. For anyone. And to be frank, you're in high school – you have no idea how difficult life can be.'

'Yeah, miss, but with all due respect, you don't know what it's like to wake up every few days and see your nationality blamed for half the street crime in New South Wales,' he argues. 'And even when you protest about it, nobody cares and nobody listens. At least in a school like this one, we're in a safe haven where we all belong.' He looks at Shehadie and quickly adds, 'Oh, sorry, *almost* all of us.'

'Mr Malouf, if you're insinuating that Mr Goldsmith is somehow less entitled to an education at this school because he has a slightly different background to you, then you're not the type of student we want here. You might want to reflect on some of the things you sing about in the school anthem on Monday mornings, or some of the Christian values of love and charity the priests talk about at Mass.'

'Miss, Zayden never sings in assembly anyway,' pipes up David Ishak.

'That's because he's always late,' Jordan Rahme calls out.

A bunch of students start laughing.

'Settle down, everyone,' Mrs Cafree admonishes. 'And get into your groups, please.'

I find myself on the affirmative side with Shehadie. Our group leader, Amanda Karam, is a nice girl who's extremely quiet. She tells us that while she's happy to lead, she doesn't want to be a speaker. After nominating three speakers, she fishes around the group for one more.

'What about you, Sophie?' she asks.

Everyone looks at me.

'Uhh, I don't think so,' I say.

'Why not?' she says. 'You're smart, I bet you'd have some insightful things to say.'

'Nah, really, I'm not confident enough. It's not my thing.'

'Fair enough. Well, you can contribute to the arguments and the research then, which we'll probably need by end of day tomorrow. The debate's going to be on Friday, so I'd like at least two days to prepare.'

'Okay, sounds good,' I say, relieved.

'So what are your arguments?' she asks.

'Yeah, Soph,' Shehadie echoes. 'What are you going to argue?'

Shite, this is awkward. How can I say what I want to say without calling my community out for being ignorant? How can I say that we need to open up to others if we want others to be open to us? That we need to be more accepting, without suggesting we compromise our strong cultural identity?

Everyone is looking at me again.

'Um, I'm not exactly sure yet. I'll have to think about it,' I say.

Lisa Nicolas, who is sitting next to Shehadie, smirks at me. 'What is there to think about?' she says. 'It's fairly straightforward. You either agree or disagree.'

'I thought you wanted arguments,' I try to defend myself. 'So I want to think of some.'

'It's not that hard to come up with a point of view,' she says. 'I personally think that opening the school to a variety of students will make things more exciting.' She looks at Shehadie and smiles. 'After all, it's not like we're all unhappy with our test case.'

'Way to make him sound like a science experiment, Lisa,' someone says. I don't know who, because Shehadie is staring at me and my cheeks are so hot I feel like I'm burning up.

'Okay, come on, guys, let's focus,' Amanda says. 'So, Sophie, arguments?'

'Oh, I don't know,' I say, exasperated. 'I can't think of anything on the spot.'

'Okay, forget it,' Amanda says. 'Anyone else have something we can work with?'

A flurry of suggestions follows and Amanda writes them down. I avoid everyone's gaze as much as I can, especially Shehadie's.

—◊—

When class is over and I'm walking out, I hear Dora tell Vanessa that she can't wait for Friday.

Zayden winks at me. 'Interesting lesson, ay, Soph? Say hi to your brother, will you.'

'Sure thing,' I say, but he doesn't hang around for my response.

When I get home and pull out my school diary, a little piece of paper falls out. It's a note, written in Shehadie's messy handwriting.

Eleanor Roosevelt once said that no one can feel invisible without their consent.

Kurt Cobain once said he'd rather be disliked for who he is than loved and respected for who he's not.

Sophie Kazzi once said that she hated feeling invisible, but when the time came for her to step up in defence of someone who thought of her as a friend, she couldn't follow through. She chose instead to be liked for who she isn't, instead of who she is – a girl who's smarter and has more decency and sense than all the rest of them put together.

So Shehadie Goldsmith wants to know: why do you let them scare you so much, Soph?

Did I mention how much I hate him getting inside my head?

17

I hate that finding my place means listening to my conscience

'That's it?' I say when my team and I meet on the morning of the debate to go over our speaking order. 'Those are our arguments?'

'Well, it's not like you volunteered anything,' Lisa points out.

'I didn't have any good ideas. I didn't think we'd be going with arguments as generic as "other cultural backgrounds are going to broaden our horizons" without explaining how or why that's even good.'

'So we should scrap them?' Amanda Karam asks me, looking frustrated.

'No,' I say, sighing. This is my fault after all. 'We just need to elaborate on them.'

'With what? The debate's after lunch,' she says.

'So? I'll skip Maths and go to the library to write something up. Let's hope to God I can deliver it okay.'

'Since when did you skip classes?' Lisa asks.

'Since now,' I say, exasperated. 'This is essential.'

'So you're going to be fourth speaker now?' Lisa says, raising her eyebrows. 'What about Shehadie?'

Shehadie puts his hands up. 'Hey, I never wanted to be fourth speaker to begin with. I'll probably be shot dead by Zayden the minute I open my mouth. By all means, let's hear what Ms Kazzi has to say.'

I glare at him just as the bell rings for morning assembly.

'Okay then, guys,' Amanda says. 'I guess I'll see you all in Society and Culture. Please bring loud voices and optimistic attitudes.'

—ɯ—

By the time the bell rings to signal the end of lunch, I'm so nervous I could throw up. I wish I'd never volunteered to be a speaker. When did I get so high and mighty with my opinions that I thought it okay to share them with an audience – especially one that's likely to be hostile?

I walk into the classroom to see Mrs Cafree sitting at the front, with four chairs on either side of her desk, facing the audience. I'm suddenly filled with dread when I see Zayden sitting in the opposite side's fourth speaker chair. Why do I have to go up against him?

When it's finally my turn to speak, I think of all the times I've been upset because of the way my community has been portrayed in the media. I think of how nice it would be to approach someone without worrying if they have a preconceived idea about me based on my looks, my surname or the suburb I live in. I think of acceptance, and what it can do for people's self-esteem, their growth and experience. I think of my parents, who want nothing but the best for others but still choose to socialise with their own kind. I think of how we're growing up in darkness, but complain because people choose to stay in the dark about us.

And I take a deep breath and say out loud what I've been thinking for a very long time.

'Ladies and gentlemen of Year Twelve, Mrs Cafree, my fellow debaters. The negative side's fourth speaker stated that keeping our school monocultural will keep our world functioning the way that it's supposed to. But I stand here before you to counter this argument, which is steeped in the ignorance we profess to be victimised by.

'Although our school has sheltered us from the racism that stems from the misrepresentation of our community – something that's been ongoing since the gang crime in south-western Sydney in the late 1990s – recent events have reminded us that ignorance of our customs and heritage is still widespread. If we go with the suggestion of our fourth speaker, that is, if we keep the world running the way he claims it's supposed to, people will continue to know nothing about us, they will continue to claim that we do not belong here because we are different.

'We'll get nowhere if we stay wrapped up in our cultural cocoon, because the ignorance will remain. Keeping our school closed off from the wider world belies the fact that Australian society is a melting pot of cultures. It keeps us in an enclave, and as long as we stay in that enclave others will continue to stereotype us.

'Hopefully, by the time we get to uni or college or TAFE or wherever, we can change that. We can go out into the world to say that we're different. But why wait till then, when we can change it now? And what better way to change it than on our own turf? Today's debate topic came out of a school fight between two boys from, for argument's sake, different cultural backgrounds. Against the backdrop of events such as the Cronulla riots and the recent Brighton Brawl, this schoolyard fight says a lot about our social attitudes.

'Today's debate is about a lot more than changing our school. When we consider the bigger picture, this argument goes to the heart of acceptance, hospitality and compassion. Our parents and grandparents left everything they'd ever known to create better lives for us. They left a country where they belonged, and made long and difficult journeys to come here, knowing that they'd be the "other". This wonderful country didn't turn them away. It opened up its homes, its hospitals, its neighbourhood communities for them. It gave them special schools to help them keep a little part of their heritage in their lives; it provided government benefits for those who are parents, or students, or elderly, or looking for work. Its justice system aims to be fair, and everyone is innocent until proven guilty.

'None of these things were available where our parents came from ... and all of these things were instituted by the "Skips" that some of us here wish to exclude. If someone doesn't want to be a part of this wonderful country with its offer of a second chance, they are more than welcome to leave. The question is, would they actually want to?

'Our school dynamics have already changed – we have a student here who forces us to put into practice what we ourselves expect from the wider community. This is our chance to give back the hospitality that has been extended to us, in the hope that one day a future generation may call it a blessing too.

'What is this situation if not an opportunity to grow, learn and prosper? Difference can make us stronger; we just have to be strong enough to accept it.'

I'm too scared to look up when I finish, but then I hear the applause and let out a sigh of relief. Mrs Cafree congratulates me on a job well done, and a few people come up to say that I've opened their eyes, which is nice, because in reality we all know that our school isn't likely to change.

'Sometimes when you talk you're nice to listen to,' a voice says behind me.

I turn around to face Shehadie. 'I'm always nice to listen to,' I counter.

'Okay then, you were especially nice to listen to today.'

'I meant what I said,' I tell him, searching his face for a clue as to what he really thinks. 'And I'm sorry for letting you down. It takes practice … this speaking up.'

'Personally, I'm a big fan of the saying that actions speak louder than words,' he says. 'It would've been nice to have a few people come to my defence when I was being taunted in the quad. But you have a wonderful way with words, and I guess they're worth listening to.'

'Thanks, Shehadie,' I say but he's already walking away.

—⟨⟨⟨—

On my way to History, I'm accosted by Zayden.

'Really, Sophie, you believe all that stuff?' he says. 'I thought you were a good Lebanese girl.'

'You know what, Zayden, I am,' I retort. 'Especially because I don't go around bragging that I'm proud of my heritage while doing nothing to promote what our heritage is really about.'

'Well, at least your brother's on side,' he says, shaking his head and walking away. 'He knows what's good for him.'

I watch him leave, mulling over his words. If what Zayden said is true, then battle lines are in place – not just at school but at home as well – and I'm not sure how ready I am for the fight.

18

I hate that I've become paranoid about my friendships falling apart

'I'm depressed,' I announce to Sue, as I flop down next to her at our lunch spot on Thursday afternoon. 'I have no idea what relevance Albert Speer has to World War II, which means I'm going to fail History. Plus, my aunty has something weird going on that she's not telling me about, and I'm bummed about it because we've always been close. I really don't need someone else abandoning me at this stage of my life. I mean, I'm a friendless girl with braces, glasses, frizzy hair, a Stone Age dad and no date to the formal. I need a life transplant, or at least a girly movie night.'

Sue takes a bite of her apple and looks at me sternly. 'Sophie, if you say you're friendless one more time, I'm going to take offence. What are we – the half-time entertainment between your old life and whatever new one you're waiting for? Just accept that we're your friends now and deal with it. Your life's not going to get much better, trust me. I have an intuition about these things.'

'Ahh, where have you been all my life?' I say, putting my arms around her. 'You're just the reality check I need right now.'

'Okay, since we're talking reality checks,' she says, shooting a cheeky glance at Nicole, 'when are you going to admit you have a crush on Shehadie?'

'Say what now?' I ask.

'Shehadie. You have a crush on him. I can practically see the butterflies in your stomach every time he walks into the room.'

I start to protest, but Sue gives me a look that's a cross between you-should-know-better-than-to-argue and I-wasn't-born-yesterday. I blush and smile.

'That's not a conversation for the quad,' I say. 'And that's all I'm saying unless there's movies and junk food involved.'

Nicole leans over me to Sue and whispers loudly, 'I think she wants to get together one night and you're not getting the hint.'

'Oh!' Sue says. 'How delayed am I! Sorry, Soph, it's because you lost me at Albert Speer and life transplants and such … But that's a great idea! We haven't had a movie or coffee night since you joined the group.'

I cross my arms and feign anger. 'You bitches have been trying to avoid hanging out with me for weeks now, but you can't avoid me anymore.'

'She's all over us like a bad smell,' Thomas says, sauntering over to join us.

'Ohhh, how exciting!' Nicole claps her hands, ignoring him. 'Let's make it a sleepover.'

'Are you guys kidding?' I exclaim. 'My dad's of the old world! The only time I'll be allowed to sleep outside our house is when I get married, and I reckon even that's open to speculation. Sorry, but it's gonna have to be a regular night with an 11 pm curfew or something.'

'What?' the girls ask in unison. 'You've never had a sleepover before?'

'Dad thinks I'll get raped if I'm not sleeping under his roof,' I say slowly. 'Or worse, that no one will marry me. Don't all wog parents think like that?'

'Only the old-fashioned ones,' Thomas says. 'Oh, there's Mrs Rivera! Sorry, guys, I need to go ask her to put up my English grade because I put a lot of effort into my assignment.'

'No, you didn't,' Sue says. 'You started it three hours before it was due and wagged Maths and Senior Science to finish it. And you only had one extra source instead of two.'

'Yeah, but she doesn't know that, does she? What she does know … no, wait, what she'll soon know is that my grandma's really sick in hospital and I'm distraught because she's my favourite relative. I've lost focus on all things that matter in my life, especially my studies.'

'I don't know how he gets away with it,' I say, pulling out my sandwiches. 'Oh gosh, mortadella again? Eeek.'

'Okay, back to the girly night,' Nicole says. 'How's tomorrow night? Should we tell the boys? Or is it strictly a female affair?'

'I can't do tomorrow night!' I whinge. 'Friday nights we have family dinners. Can you guys do Saturday?'

'Yep,' they reply in unison.

'I'm sensing we need to get to the bottom of this Sophie character, Nic,' Sue says, tapping her chin. 'We'll need all the girl power that we can muster. Girly films, music, popcorn, marshmallows and manicures.' She counts them off on her fingers.

'Ooooh,' I say happily. 'Sounds like the ultimate female affair. I'm VERY excited.'

—m—

The ultimate female affair ends up being crashed by Thomas and Jacob, who turn up at Sue's house about half an hour before I do and pretend like they had no idea what was planned for the evening.

'I couldn't get them to leave,' Sue explains as I wave to Dad from her front door so he can establish that a girl has answered and that she looks about my age. 'Thomas even brought some chick flicks. This night's going to be a lot more exciting than you may have planned, my dear.'

'Sounds fab,' I say. 'After all, I need it.'

Three and a half hours later, I'm lying on Sue's living room floor eating raspberry twists. Thomas is sitting on the couch, Nicole is half-asleep with her head in his lap, and Sue is sitting on the floor with her knees pulled up in front of her.

'Okay, Soph,' she says, 'you've managed to avoid telling us for long enough. So … what's going on with you and Shehadie?'

I become fascinated with a spot on the carpet. 'I don't know what you're talking about. We're just friends.'

'Yeah, right,' scoffs Thomas. 'You've suddenly started speaking up in his defence, you twirl your hair in this pathetic little way when you talk to him, and last week I could've sworn that you purposely wore a black bra under a white shirt and put fake tan on your legs and then put them on the desk in front of him.'

'Do you ever tire of exaggerating?' I ask. 'I don't know what the hell you're talking about. It's winter – I've been wearing tights since May.'

'My point exactly,' he says. 'Girls like Vanessa get what they want because they actually do those things. You just make a sob-story musical out of everything and eat your pain's worth in ice-cream.'

Sue and I stare at him.

'Speaking of which, you're getting a little chunky in the thigh area, you may want to lay off the sweet stuff,' he says, plucking the raspberry twist out of my hands and shoving it into his mouth.

'Honestly, Tom, what's the matter with you?' Sue asks, laughing. 'But seriously, Soph, don't tell me you're not interested.'

I feel trapped. 'Okay, I'm interested,' I admit. 'But what's the point? Have you seen the girls he's friends with on Facebook? Or some of the photos he's been tagged in? Not only do I have to compete with beautiful blondes with tanned legs and not a blemish in sight, but I also have a very enticing angry Lebanese dad and a curfew that wouldn't have seemed out of place in Nazi Germany. And both of us have the wrath of Vanessa and Zayden and God knows who else hanging over us. So it's not like we could ever have a functioning relationship.'

'But you're never going to know unless you suss it out, Soph,' Thomas says.

'I can't,' I say, shrugging. 'That's what I mean. There's too much going against us already. Plus, he's been weird with me lately, even after the debate.' I sigh, looking at their sympathetic faces. 'I honestly thought this year would be different. I wanted a date to the formal, to get ready with Dora, to have someone tell me I look beautiful.'

Sue hugs me, then rests her head on my shoulder. 'It's okay, Sophie.'

'In some respects, it's more than okay,' I admit. 'Like, I'm friends with you guys now, and that makes me really happy. Plus, Thomas tells me I'm beautiful every single day, even if it is in his own twisted way.'

We giggle and put on another DVD.

'Jacob, stop watching the football and get in here,' Sue yells. 'And bring some Doritos – they're on the kitchen bench.' She sits back down and passes me a block of chocolate. 'Two hours till your dad comes to take you home, Soph. We'd better make the most of it.'

Home. Funny, that's where it feels like I am right now.

19

I hate realising I'm my own worst enemy

Term three is a mash-up of frantic preparations for our final assessments, hopeless cramming and late-night study sessions. The senior boys' football team makes it to the semi-finals of the Catholic Boys Athletics Association (CBAA) Rugby League Cup, and Sister Magdalena orders all students from Years Ten, Eleven and Twelve to attend to show their support.

I sit next to Thomas on the way to the match, and he manages to keep a completely straight face as he explains that Jacob has caught herpes from the old lady who teaches him violin and will be 'resigning' from school.

'Where do you get your material?' I ask. 'Do you think I was born yesterday? I happen to know that Jacob's actually getting treated for a rare but highly contagious ear fungus that he caught after years of listening to your bullshit.'

'Well, at least we're all accustomed to listening to bullshit,' he replies. 'Because if we weren't, your constant protestations about your lack of interest in one Shehadie Goldsmith could actually do our ears some damage.'

'Oh, you smug son of a very nice lady,' I say, elbowing him and laughing. 'You know there's nothing going on there. But seriously, isn't it cute that Jacob's gone in early with the team to cover the game for the yearbook?'

'Yeah, Sister Magdalena was so impressed she'll probably give him a special word of thanks at the school assembly we'll have after we lose today. Which is great for Jacob – those years of practising photography by taking photos of girls without their knowledge is about to pay off.'

'Oh, for the love of God,' Sue pipes up from the seat behind us. 'Would you two cut him some slack? Soph, I expected better from you.'

I shrug. 'What can I say? Tom's pathetic sense of humour is catching.'

We tumble out of the bus laughing about how none of us understands football and devising a plan to go shopping in Chinatown instead. But, being the nerds we are, we all know we'll never go through with it. We're too scared of the Sister Magdalena.

By the time we've filed into our grade's allotted section in the stands, there's a potent mix of excitement and tension in the air. Nicole grabs onto both Sue and me, and semi-screeches something so fast that all I register is 'Oh my God', 'Shehadie' and 'old school'. Sue holds Nicole by the shoulders and tells her to calm down. It works: Nicole slows down enough for us to understand what she's saying.

'Oh my God, guys, you are not going to believe this,' she hisses. 'We can give up the pretence of going to Chinatown now, because the game's about to get super interesting. The whole day, actually. I mean, not because I didn't want to go to Chinatown and all, but –'

'Nicole!' Thomas snaps. 'Would you hurry the hell up and get to the point? My pubes are going grey waiting for you!'

'Ewww,' we reply in unison.

'Seriously, what's going on?' he demands.

'Well, remember how Charlie Nehme went to Lebanon in the holidays, and how he missed out on the first two weeks of school?' she says.

We nod, waiting for the dramatic bit to begin.

'Well, according to the rules of the CBACCC or whatever the hell it's called, he can't play in the final because he hasn't officially been part of the team for long enough.'

'That's crazy,' I say. 'He's been playing in both the league and soccer teams since they introduced rep sport to the school.'

'Yeah, but rules are rules,' she says. 'So because he's not playing –'

'Our team's one man down and Thomas has to play?' Sue says mischievously.

Thomas gives Sue a death stare. 'Heart attacks are a serious issue.'

Nicole shakes her head. 'No, it means that Shehadie has to play in his place! Which is bad because –'

'It's going to give them more of a reason to hate him,' I finish for her. 'How awful.'

'No, Soph,' Nicole says. 'It's bad because our school's playing against his old one. That's dramatic enough, but it gets better, because Vanessa says that she's heard our boys are going to alienate him from the game – they think he's going to try to throw the game so his buddies from his old school win.'

'That's ridiculous,' Thomas says. 'Shehadie hasn't been made to feel welcome at CSC, but that doesn't mean he's low enough to throw a game.'

'Thomas is right,' I chime in. 'He's an honourable guy. Vanessa's probably being an idiot, but no one can see through it because … well, she's Vanessa.'

The others laugh.

'Surely our boys won't really alienate him from the game,' I say. 'That would be crazy. Plus, they'll get in trouble – they need him. Coach Todd and Mr Shora would never let them live it down.'

'Wake up, Sophie,' Sue says, gesturing to everyone around us. 'Look at the way they treat the guy at school. They're not gonna care if it costs them a game, they're more concerned with putting up some dumb wall between him and the rest of the school. It's all about reputation for them – they just want to prove a point.'

I roll my eyes. 'What idiots. Do you think we should warn a teacher or something?'

'Nah,' Sue replies. 'I reckon it'd make the situation worse. Let's just sit here and wish we were somewhere else. This game is gonna be like a Band-Aid – the sooner it's off, the better.'

As Sue finishes speaking, the teams run out onto the field and hundreds of teenage girls hold their breath. It's funny – we ignore the guys most of the time at school, but the minute they change into some sort of sports uniform they're suddenly worth checking out.

The whistle blows, signalling the start of the first half. Nothing much happens for the first twenty minutes or so. I spot Shehadie sitting on the bench and wonder if he's not a very good player.

'He's quite good, actually,' Thomas says, reading my mind. 'But Coach Todd's all about fairness and equality and team bonding, yada yada yada, so he likes to give everyone a turn. I reckon he'll go on soon, so yes, girl, you will get to check out his rear in action.'

I want to smack him, but I can't help smiling at his fairly accurate assumption.

'Fat lot of good fairness and team bonding are going to do now,' Sue says, twirling a strand of her wild curls.

Dad and Andrew aren't into sports and I haven't been exposed to much football, so I'm surprised at how interesting I find the game. By the time Shehadie runs onto the field, Sue, Nicole and I have figured out how the rules work. In his footy gear, Shehadie is an absolute hottie. Even watching him run is a turn-on, but the fact that I'm thinking this makes me want to throw up. Luckily the others are too absorbed in the game to notice, even when Shehadie cops a particularly vicious tackle and I leap to my feet in worry. I quickly sit back down, my cheeks burning.

When the half-time whistle sounds, the score is 14–10 and our school is one try and one conversion away from the lead. As the teams scurry back to their benches, I find I want to discuss the possibilities for the second half with anyone who'll listen.

Just then Rita Malkoun walks past with Vanessa, no doubt en route to the toilets to check out their hair. They look my way and giggle. Thomas turns to me and his face says it all: why aren't you standing up for yourself? So I do.

'What the hell is your problem?' I ask Rita, ignoring Vanessa. She might be the Queen Bee, but her level of bitchiness is nowhere near her deputy's.

Rita laughs again and answers without looking at me, trying to make me feel even more worthless. 'Don't worry, Sophie, we weren't laughing at you. Believe it or not, there are better things to laugh about. Although come to think of it, the way you wear that uniform leaves a lot to be desired. What year is this – 1954?'

'I can't believe Dora's hanging out with that girl!' I say, gritting my teeth as she walks off. 'I don't know why she's being such a bitch all of a sudden – she was perfectly happy ignoring me up until this year. It's not like I have anything she or Vanessa wants – they did get custody of my best friend, after all. Or *former* best friend,' I add.

'Earth to Sophie,' Thomas replies. 'They're ignoring you because a hot piece of intriguing new boy only has eyes for you. Don't you know they want a monopoly on any new people of interest that come to our school?'

'That's absolute rubbish,' I say. 'They couldn't give a shit about Shehadie – he's the *foreigner*, remember?' I put finger quotation marks around the word.

'I'm aware of that,' he says. 'But every guy who's ever set foot in this school has made a beeline for them, and he's the first one who hasn't. You might only be friends with him because of work, but he pays you all the attention that he's not paying them. Rita especially can't stand it. She knows the boys are only interested in Vanessa anyway, so she feels really undermined that as the second-most popular girl she's still a nobody. Even worse, the person she thinks is a nobody has a cute guy after her, even if – and I mean *if* – it's only for friendship.'

'That makes no sense,' I say, even though on some level I can see his point. I just don't want to admit it.

He takes my hand and tugs me back towards our seats. When we sit down, I put my feet up on the chair in front. He smiles at me and then looks away, shaking his head.

'What?' I ask.

'Rita does have another thing to be jealous of,' he says. 'You have the hottest legs in our grade. It's a downright shame that your netball skirt is double the length of everyone else's.'

I lean into him and sigh. 'I can't wait to get out of this shallow school and into the big wide world. And don't make fun of my skirt. What's the point of wearing it short if I need to keep tugging at it, or whining about how I can't bend down to pick my bag up? The school needs to hurry up and get us some shorts for netball.'

'That'll never happen, baby,' he says. He drops his voice as if he's about to tell me some deep dark secret. 'They're very unflattering and unladylike.'

'So, my kind of style, ay?' I say, giggling.

He shrugs. 'Come to think of it, girl, people are gonna laugh at your clothes whether you're in school or not. Now come on, there's a game we gotta finish watching.'

The second half kicks off and we wait to see the drama unfold. It doesn't take long to realise that the boys on our team are choosing to make the worst kind of plays instead of passing the ball to Shehadie. It's as if he isn't even on the field. To make things worse, the boys from his old school keep taunting him about his new suburb.

'Gonna get any gangsta tattoos now you're living in the ghetto?'

'Got yourself a dark, hairy girlfriend yet?'

172

'The move must've been convenient for you, Goldie – probably got the head of a drug ring living next door now. You got easy access at all hours of the night?'

'And one of the busiest cop stations around just in case he blows up again, right?'

From the stand, I can see Shehadie's face redden. Sue and I look at each other, wondering what the hell the taunts mean. Even Thomas seems confused. Even more distressing is the fact that the coach and teachers from the other school must be able to hear what's going on, but they don't do anything.

The game goes on, its score still 14–10.

Nicole announces she's bored and starts filing her nails. She isn't bored for long, though, because a fight breaks out on the field. The ref calls time out, but by now both teams are caught up in it, except for Shehadie, who appears torn between the two sides. But then someone says something to him and he's in it too, and all I can see is a group of teenage boys punching and shoving.

'Who'd have thought the Aussie bloke was gonna fight on our side?' someone behind me says.

'Are they really that surprised?' Sue asks, leaning over to me.

'Evidently so,' Thomas scoffs.

Eventually the fight is over, and although both coaches look mad, they don't punish any of the players. Zayden kicks the ground in front of him. He's standing in a little huddle with his friends, while Shehadie's a few metres away, on his own. My heart seems to stop as Zayden starts walking over to him. But to my surprise, Zayden sticks out his hand and they shake. A moment later, the ref blows the whistle and the game gets going again.

By the last ten minutes, it's obvious our team has accepted defeat. But I don't care. I'm just happy that after months of taunting, it seems like Shehadie's finally being accepted into the fold. I'm chatting to Nicole when suddenly Thomas grabs me by the shoulders and turns me towards the field. Shehadie has possession of the ball and is powering towards the try line. Ten metres out, he's about to be tackled by the opposition when he passes to Zayden, who manages to cross the line to score a try. The two boys look at each other for a second, unsure what to do, but then they're surrounded by the rest of the team, jumping up and down and hugging them.

In the stands, we're on our feet as we watch Daniel Abboud successfully kick a goal for conversion. And just like that, we're in the lead with only a couple of minutes to go.

When the full-time whistle sounds, there are loud cheers from our side of the stands as we realise the CSC boys have made it to the grand final.

'Wow, talk about a dramatic game,' Sue says. 'At least it all worked out in the end. Though I wonder how long it'll last.'

'I don't think Zayden and Shehadie are going to be the best of friends,' I reply. 'But at least Zayden won't keep being horrible to him now.'

I see Shehadie separate himself from the team to go talk to a bunch of spectators from his old school. There are a few very pretty girls in the group and they giggle and hug him excitedly. A tall, attractive blonde throws her arms around him, and he gives her a kiss on the cheek.

Rita sees me watching and sends me an evil little smile. Next to her, Dora shakes her head, looking apologetic.

Sue sees me staring and tugs at me gently. 'Come on, Soph, time to go,' she whispers, reaching for my hand.

'Do you reckon he was popular at his old school?' I ask, not taking my eyes off him and the girl.

'From what we're seeing now, I think that's an understatement,' she replies, pulling me away.

I take one final look and follow her, wondering if I've stuffed things up with Shehadie for the sake of a few people at school who haven't proved their worth in all the years I've known them. What does that say about me? That I'm weak? A follower? That I've thrown his friendship back in his face? That I've done the same thing to him that I hated Dora for doing to me?

Shehadie and I have a lot in common: we're two peas in a really big pod of indifferent people. We can talk about absolutely anything and still pretend to hate each other, make really dumb jokes and still laugh, tell each other how boring our weekends were with their Saturday chores and supermarket visits with our mother or grandmother and still be interested. I can be myself around him.

I sigh as the realisation hits me. I'm in love with Shehadie Goldsmith, even though I don't want to be. Things were easier when I was in love with Zayden Malouf, the guy who can speak my father's language, who understands all of our traditions. Zayden, or at least some version of him, is the right guy on paper. But that train of thought just reminds me that it's time I got my head out of books and started living a real life.

20

I hate it when I give a part of myself away ... with no guarantee of the outcome

Even though I haven't spoken to Leila for a couple of weeks, I still feel grateful to her every time I go to work. It feels good to be able to whinge about customers for a change instead of always whingeing about my life. Especially when I'm on front desk and have to deal with people telling ridiculous lies in order to get refunds and listen to the heated arguments about what can and can't be exchanged.

Shehadie is on front desk with me today, and by the end of the shift he's made me laugh so hard my stomach hurts. I can see why they put him here – his easygoing, blokey nature soothes customers who are angry about a faulty appliance or mismatched curtain packs. He has an innate ability to calm people down, not to mention those amazing eyes that practically intoxicate customers into submission.

As we file the end-of-day paperwork, I realise that I've begun to relish moments alone with him. Right now he's poking fun at just how quickly my friendship with Dora broke down as soon as she got a taste of Vanessa and Rita's style of popularity.

'The sad thing is, they're the only ones who buy into it,' he says. 'I bet you eighty per cent of the people in our grade couldn't care less about them, but they can't be bothered changing the status quo so they don't put them in their place.'

I shrug. 'I don't know, but to be honest, I don't think I even blame her anymore. And I really don't want to whinge about it, either – I need to remind myself that I'm not the teenager of the year, you know? There are heaps of girls my age going through the same teenage crap – well, not exactly the same, but similar.'

'As in, they don't have Dictator Dad?' he says, smiling.

'Exactly right!' I laugh. 'I'm pretty sure that all my teenage melodrama can be channelled into something that will benefit me in the long run. I just need to work out what that something is.'

'Well, you're not going to find it studying accounting, that's for sure,' he says. 'I don't understand why you're even going to preference that. Haven't you looked through the UAC guide? There's got to be a course that'll harness all that pent-up cynicism you wear as your badge.'

'I don't think I need career advice from a guy who claims he doesn't want to make plans for tomorrow, let alone next year.'

'Sophie,' he says, 'my mother died in her prime. There's a reason I don't make plans – I don't believe in them. You don't know what the next minute has in store for you, so why set yourself up for disappointment.'

'There's nothing wrong with being optimistic,' I say.

'Right, because the girl who spends her days tabulating everything that's wrong with the world and listening to teen-angst music is suddenly the poster girl for optimism.' He laughs. 'I can just picture you a year from now, sitting in an accounting lecture with all these nerds, bored out of your brain but still wearing that defiant cloak of sarcasm and invisibility, because deep down you're afraid that someone will see through it to the looker that you are and break your heart.'

I stare at him, bewildered. 'Say what now?'

'You heard me. Behind that facade about being all hatey and mean, you're just afraid someone will notice you, fall for you and then let you down by not being on your level. You don't give people a chance because you won't even trust yourself with one.'

'Shut up,' I scoff, rifling through a trolley filled with stuff that needs to be returned to the shelves or to the supplier.

Just then, Casey waltzes in, holding a copy of *Girlfriend* and followed by Jordan.

'Aren't you too old to be reading that?' Jordan asks her. 'And, more importantly, too old to be doing those silly quizzes?'

'It's a good mag and the quizzes are fun,' she says. 'Come on, we'll all do one.'

'Um, did you actually buy that, or are you borrowing again?' Shehadie says sternly.

'I'll put it back straight after,' she says, hands together as if in prayer. 'I promise.'

Shehadie shakes his head and rolls his eyes, and I wonder how it feels to be caught between being their friend and their team leader.

'Okay,' Casey says. 'You've been dating your crush for a few months now and his bestie tells you he's going to ask you to ...' She stops and looks at me. 'Ah, these are silly, let's not worry about it,' she says, her face reddening slightly.

'No way!' Jordan says, snatching the magazine off her. 'You can't just start then stop. I'll do it.' He clears his throat and starts reading aloud.

Casey mouths the word 'sorry' to me, but I don't understand until Jordan finishes the rest of the sentence.

'... his bestie tells you he's going to ask you to *do it*, but you're not ready. What do you tell him?' He looks up at us, smirking. 'It wouldn't matter what she told me,' he says, 'because I'd be outta there. A guy has needs, you know.'

I can feel my face getting hot. I'm uncomfortable having this conversation, and everyone except Jordan senses it.

'You know how it is, man, don't you?' he goes on, turning to Shehadie and elbowing him.

'Not really,' Shehadie responds. 'I guess if I really liked her, I'd wait. Some things are worth waiting for.'

His frankness stuns us all and we're silent. Shehadie shrugs like he doesn't care.

We're saved by Casey's phone ringing. 'Woohoo, my brother's here,' she says. 'Finally I get to leave this dump and go home. No offence, guys.'

I laugh. 'None taken. Enjoy your night.'

Jordan follows her, leaving Shehadie and me alone. My curiosity gets the better of me.

'Did you mean that?' I ask. 'What you just said about waiting?'

'Well, I've read enough good fiction to know that there's lust and then there's love.'

What does that even mean? Why couldn't he just say yes or no like a normal person? Or is this how he gets all the girls to fall for him?

I feel proud of myself for seeing right through him, until he reaches over to get the stapler and his hand brushes against my waist. My breath catches. He's looking at me intently and holding his position close to me. I can smell his aftershave and suddenly I'm dying and I don't know why. I was in love with Zayden Malouf for so long, but this much nerdier guy is making my heart beat faster than Zayden ever did.

I need to break the intensity, so I laugh at him and say something stupid. 'You're weird. I mean, you're eighteen – you're genetically programmed to want to get physical. As far as I know, only boys who pray the rosary want to wait.'

He smirks and moves away, not looking at me as he staples a bunch of receipts to the end-of-day paperwork.

'I see you've had your head in the health books – shame you're not doing PDHPE for the HSC.'

I make a face at him and he laughs.

'Well, you did say it yourself,' I point out. 'Need I remind you of our conversation about *The Bronze Horseman*?'

His voice softens. 'See, I don't even need to say anything. You already know it all.'

'Do I?' I ask quietly.

'Does it matter what I think or say anyway? Really?'

I shrug.

'I don't pray the rosary and I don't know if I want to wait,' he says. 'But like I said, it all depends on the girl. I might think the same way that Jordan does only to find a game-changer right under my nose, right?'

He winks at me and I don't know how to respond. I'm freaked out about the way he's looking at me. So I just stand there, trying to keep my cool, even though I could melt under his gaze.

'I want to wait until I'm married,' I tell him, because I can't think of anything else to say. But as soon as it's out there I want to take it back.

But he responds in a way that only Shehadie Goldsmith would. 'Because you want to, or because that's what's expected?'

I'm impressed, not only because he's questioning my motivation, but also because he makes *me* want to question it.

'Because that's what God expects,' I say finally.

'Again with something that someone else wants and not something you've put thought into,' he says.

'God isn't *someone*, thank you very much.'

He puts the paperwork down and turns to me, speaking slowly. 'But someone told you they're the rules that God expects you to follow. You have to find your own reason in the rules, Soph, because only then will you be a hundred and ten per cent happy with your decision and actually see it through. Otherwise it'll stop mattering.'

I resent his tone for a second because it makes me feel like a fool. But then I stop and consider what he's really saying.

'I don't know,' I say. 'It just seems less complicated that way. There's reason in the rules, right? No STIs, no pregnancies, no one bitching about what I've done and who with. And certainly not the stress about who I might be wasting it on. If a guy loves me enough to wait for me, then I know that if we get married he's not going to walk out at the first sign of trouble.'

He looks at me, one eyebrow raised. 'That's not the reason and we both know it.'

'Fine,' I say in a huff. 'Because it's mine, and I want to give it away when I've made a solid commitment that I believe is unbreakable.' I turn away to tidy the desk, unable to look at him. 'To me, it's an actual part of myself, and I want to wait until I'm married because I want to believe that the guy I marry deserves it. It's romanticised and perhaps a little clichéd and all the more outdated, but I guess that's the reason I'm content with.'

I feel his breath on my neck as he leans in to whisper in my ear and I think I could die on the spot.

'I reckon I could live with that,' he murmurs.

And then he's back doing his job like we didn't just have the biggest conversation *ever*, and I envy him for being so cool when I feel like I've just given my soul away.

I play the conversation over and over in my head on the way home, increasingly mortified and confused. Somehow I'm certain that things between us will never be the same again ... and I'm not sure how ready I am for things to change.

21

I hate it when I'm caught completely off guard

As the year moves beyond July, people in my grade start turning eighteen. Dad is more lenient about parties that are held in the home of the birthday girl or boy, because they're local, he knows the parents will be there, and the parties are on private property. I suppose the fact that he can figure out what village a person is from based on their last name also helps.

One Saturday night I find myself heading to Joseph El-Bashir's party with Sue, Nicole, Thomas and Jacob. Dad lets me go in Jacob's car because we're a group, which is ironic because Jacob has decided that tonight is the night he'll do something radical, which will probably turn out to be driving all of us home after curfew on his P-plates. Considering we're all goody two-shoes at heart, we get a thrill out of pretending it's actually going to happen, all the while knowing that Sue will get bored an hour into the party and go home, and the rest of us will likely leave separately. I laugh to myself as I think how everyone in our class, and perhaps even our teachers, assumes that Sue is an uncool nerd, when actually she's the coolest person I know. Sue is top of our grade and incredibly smart, and the only reason she comes to these things in the first place is because her mum makes her.

'Hey, Sue,' I call out from the front seat without turning around. I'm looking in the mirror for the seventeenth time since Jacob picked us up. 'What time do you have to stay till tonight?'

I see her roll her eyes in the mirror. 'Ten thirty,' she replies.

'How come your mum's downgraded from eleven?' asks Jacob.

'Now that I'm eighteen and involved in student politics, she knows I'm getting some socialising done elsewhere so she's happy.'

'Aww, that means one less person to break P-plate legislation with me,' Jacob says.

'So whose party are we at tonight?' Sue asks.

'Do you really have no idea?' says Nicole. She shakes her head and smiles. 'Not that I'd have you any other way.'

Jacob parks the car almost a block away and we walk up a laneway that leads into the backyard. Joseph's clearly already drunk and Sue makes a face when she sees him.

'It's his eighteenth,' Jacob says, mocking her. 'Get over it, he's legal.'

'Yes, legally an idiot,' she says. 'He couldn't even understand my two-word greeting: Happy and Birthday.'

'And he dropped his present on the floor. Twice,' I point out.

'Whatevs,' Jacob says. 'There's just no pleasing you women.'

I look around the yard and see Zayden laughing with Dora and Rita. I wonder why Vanessa isn't with them. But it isn't Vanessa I'm searching for.

Jacob leans in and whispers in my ear. 'He's here. Can you relax and have fun now?'

'Maybe,' I say, smiling.

He gives my shoulder an affectionate squeeze, and I'm so thankful I don't have to use up my energy explaining or denying anything to my friends, because they already know how I'm feeling.

Suddenly I spot him, in a corner of the yard, looking better than I could ever have imagined, in dark jeans, grey vans and a simple pale blue T-shirt. He knows that he's been busted staring at me and his cheeks turn a light pink, which makes him even better-looking and I hate him for it. He smirks at me as he takes a sip of his beer, and I know that he's pretending to listen to whatever Georgina Simons and Katia Akkari are saying to him. I curse myself for being jealous of them.

I do my best to mingle, but it takes too much energy so I go inside to feign interest in the TV. At ten, Sue comes over to tell me she's leaving. I beg her to stay a little while longer.

'Seriously, Soph, I can't be bothered,' she says. 'Nicole's still here with her cousins from Mackillop, so you're not totally alone. I think they're dancing outside. You should totally go out there and hang with them instead of sitting in here and pretending you're watching the football.'

'I don't know,' I say. 'The music's so loud I can't handle it.'

'Soph, it's like you're seventeen going on seventy. What's wrong with you?'

'Says the girl who has to be bribed to stay at a party?' I say, hugging her goodbye.

We laugh and she promises to call tomorrow.

I make my way outside, and grab a Vodka Cruiser before heading to the darkest part of the yard and leaning against the fence. Out of the corner of my eye I see a guy in Year Eleven making out with some chick from another school, so I inch along the fence a little to stand by a group that I know won't talk to me. I scan the party for Jacob, but it's Shehadie who comes over to stand next to me.

'No, I don't want to dance, and yes, someone's sitting there,' I say, pointing to a chair beside me.

'Should you be drinking that?' he asks, nodding towards the bottle in my hand.

'Probably not. But it's my second one, and I don't plan on stopping until I've tried all the flavours.'

'Wow,' he says, placing one arm on the fence and leaning in closer. I'm sure I see some girls swooning across the yard. 'The world can barely handle you sober. Imagine the personality traits that'll shine through if you're drunk? Oh, the horror!' He feigns fear.

'What world, Shehadie?'

'This world,' he says, indicating himself.

'So you're the world now, are you?'

'Your world, for sure, but you'll realise that eventually.'

'Do you ever get sick of your own smugness?' I ask.

'Not a chance, baby.'

I smile and take another sip of my drink. 'Shouldn't you be hanging around with people who appreciate your company a little more?'

I don't want him to leave, though, and I think he knows it. I guess this is the only way we know how to be with each other.

'Maybe,' he says, shrugging. 'But I doubt they'd benefit from my charm and good looks as much as you will.'

I nearly choke on my drink and spit some out.

'Classy,' he says. 'Would've been really good if some of it had landed on Rita. I'd love to see you in a fight. With all that angst, you could really do some damage.'

I shoot him a look.

'Just like the damage you did in the debate,' he goes on. 'It was good to hear your real voice in class for a change.'

'Somehow I don't think everyone shares that opinion.'

'That's because they can't see past their own noses.'

I'm quiet. He busts me staring at Zayden and I look away.

'Why him, Soph?' he asks. 'He's so not right for you.'

I have to hand it to him: he's honest about what he thinks. I don't want to tell him I've already gone off Zayden and have the hots for him, partly because it would complicate what we have, partly because I don't want to believe it, and mostly because I wouldn't know what to do if he felt the same way. So instead I reply with my usual stupid banter.

'How can you presume to know what's right for me? You haven't known me that long.'

'I feel like I've known you my whole life,' he says simply. 'And I know he's beneath you.'

I swallow and look up at him. He's gazing at me intently, and this time it's my face that goes red. I don't know what to say, so I fold my arms and stare out at the dance floor again. Shehadie looks defeated.

But then Pitbull's 'Give Me Everything' comes on and I take it as a sign, because the beat makes me feel blissfully crazy when I dance and gives me a confidence I don't ordinarily have.

'Okay, Mr Smugness,' I say, turning to face him and stretching out my hand. 'Dance with me.'

My head is saying, 'What are you doing, fool?' but my heart is beating so fast and Shehadie is gazing at me with a strange mixture of fascination and confusion. And then we're in the middle of the dance floor and I'm miming the words and dancing like I'm in some sort of video clip, all the while wondering if it's my illegal consumption of alcohol that's ignited the confidence in me … but not caring.

Based on his bookishness, I'd figured that Shehadie wasn't going to be what a dancing queen's dreams were made of, but he moves really well. It must be the wog in him, I think, but I'm still surprised. And then I remember how he told me I need to stop stereotyping people and I curse him for always being one step ahead of me.

He holds my hand and twirls me around, and for once I feel like the leading lady of a movie instead of one of the stage crew, and it makes me smile so much that my face hurts.

It's hot and I'm clammy and sweaty, but I don't want to be anywhere else, and I think it's the same for him. He looks impressed and I love that I can make him feel that way. For once I feel like somebody worth seeing, and I wonder what has become of the girl who was content to live her life in the shadows.

Then the song ends … and I'm back to being me. I turn to walk away, but Shehadie isn't having a bar of it. He pulls me back towards him and kisses me, right there in the middle of the dance floor, in front of all those girls who've been checking him out all night and all those boys who probably wanted to kill him. And it's a great kiss.

'Wow,' I say, in shock.

'I know,' he says. 'I'm good.'

I narrow my eyes at him, and he laughs and leads me away down the driveway so we can talk.

'Why would you do that?' I ask, looking at the floor.

His face goes red. 'I'm sorry, Soph,' he says, retreating. He's quiet for a second and then he puts his hands in his pockets. 'But fuck, you're confusing.'

I wait expectantly.

'Like seriously,' he says. 'You're always harping on about how you're invisible and how nobody notices you and the whole time I'm paying you all this attention and you couldn't give a shit ... I mean, what's the point? Games are fun, but eventually they have to go somewhere, and I know you probably think I'm an arsehole, but I guess I just thought ...'

And then I kiss him. It takes a moment to register what I've done, and even though he's a great kisser I stop and pull back, embarrassed.

'You're right,' I say, going bright red. 'I'm sorry. I shouldn't have given you mixed messages.'

He bends down to look me in the eye. 'If this is how you apologise, you can give me as many mixed messages as you want,' he says, smiling.

I bite my lip. 'I'm kind of embarrassed.'

'Why? This is normal. It happens all the time.'

'Not to girls like me. To guys like you probably, but not with girls like me.'

'That's why I like you. And I don't want this ... I mean us, to stop tonight. I just hope you actually remember this conversation because it's awkward enough telling you once that I like you. Can you imagine how bad it'd be if you're actually drunk right now and won't remember it tomorrow?'

'It would be just your luck,' I say, smiling at him.

—∽∽—

When we return to the backyard, Jacob and Thomas grin at me, nodding their heads. We all gather around Joseph as he cuts the cake, with me standing in front of Shehadie and next to Jacob, Thomas, Nicole and her cousins. I think about how great the night has been, and shiver a little from the cold. A second later, Shehadie is rubbing his hands up and down my arms. It's a small gesture but it makes me ecstatic, because I've stared at those perfectly tanned arms for so long and now they are giving me a comfort I've needed for even longer.

Later, when I'm ready to head off with Thomas and Jacob, Shehadie grabs me by the hand. 'Why don't you just let me take you home?' he asks.

I give him a look that says, 'I'm not that kind of girl' and he knows immediately what I'm on about.

'No silly stuff,' he says, putting his hands up in front of him. 'Surfer's honour.'

'Do surfies even have honour?' I ask. 'Haven't you read *Puberty Blues*? Plus, I'm pretty sure you were drinking beer earlier.'

He laughs. 'Yes, I suppose walking you home is a bad idea … I totally forgot I didn't drive here. I only live in the next street.' He points in one direction, then turns around and points again, pretending to be confused.

I laugh. 'I have to go. We'll talk later.'

He waves goodbye, and I think about him all the way home. Finally I get to feel something that I don't have to share with anyone. Something that's all mine, something that's amazing. I fall asleep thinking of sweet kisses and hugs and Shehadie's strong tanned arms. Forget ignorance, I think. This is what bliss is all about.

22

I hate that heartache is always around the corner

When I wake up the next morning I'm still smiling. It had never been my plan to fall for Shehadie Goldsmith, but now that I have I can't believe how much time I wasted pining after Zayden Malouf. I laugh at the fact that, for once in my life, the thing that went wrong has actually been the right thing after all.

I'm supposed to spend the day studying, but my mind is too keyed up to concentrate. I keep reliving the party over and over, wondering at what point I transformed from the shy, awkward girl into the girl who asked the boy to dance, and then let him kiss her in the middle of a dance floor … with other people around.

Even my History essay and its confusing questions about Albert Speer and the Nazis can't dampen my spirits, and I find myself checking my phone every twenty minutes for messages from Shehadie. He's probably at work. We've been on different shifts lately, thanks to my request for some time off to study.

So far I've only had one message from him, a few minutes after I got home on Friday night.

Hope u got home safe. Can I call u this wknd?
Goodnight. Mr Smugness x

Evidently, I'm not the only person thinking about what happened last night, because Jacob sends me a direct message on Facebook congratulating me for doing something out of the ordinary.

It seems that everyone's abandoning study today in favour of some social networking. People's status updates and comments are all about what a great party it was, and there are photos of Joseph, the cake, and some dude in Year Eleven lying in the corner of the yard trashed and totally unaware he's going to be the butt of every senior joke for the next three months.

Vanessa posts a note titled 'Guess Who', which comes through on my feed. I click on the thread to see a bullet list of gossipy observations from the party, thinly veiled in humour, but no doubt intended to dent the self-esteem of everyone involved. We're meant to guess the girl who spent the entire night behind the shed with a guy from another school, the guy who spewed in the bathroom and went home early embarrassed, the girl who wore a disastrous outfit, and ... the two social pariahs who became the objects of one another's desire.

Oh. My. God. She can't be serious.

Already people are commenting or inserting smileys and LOLs in the comments section.

My phone rings. It's Sue. She must have been expecting an onslaught of whingeing from me because straight away she tells me to calm down and relax, that no one will know that Vanessa was talking about me and Shehadie.

'Heaps of people were messing around,' she says. 'Don't you remember Sally and Diana's tacky dirty dancing? I'm surprised that didn't make the list. Oh yes, wait, it's because they're her friends.'

'But, Sue –' I start.

'Need I remind you that she classifies everyone who isn't in her group a social pariah? Unfortunately, because she's Queen Bee people listen to her. Still, no one's really going to know who she's referring to.'

'Are you sure?' I say. 'I mean, not that I care, but I'm just so over her dumb antics. Who the hell does she think she is?'

'I know,' Sue says. 'But who cares? You totally got the boy. I'm so happy for you! Now you can stop pining.'

'Me? Pine? NEVER,' I say, feigning outrage.

We both start laughing, and then I hear her gasp.

'Sue?' I ask. 'Sue, are you there? What's wrong?'

'Um, Soph,' she says, her tone hesitant. 'Are you in front of your computer?'

'No, I'm on my bed. Why?'

She's silent.

'Why, Sue?' I ask again, concerned.

'Go refresh the screen,' she whispers.

I bolt for my computer, and it seems like an eternity waiting for it to refresh.

'Can't you just tell me what it is?' I ask, exasperated.

'No, honey, I can't. Just scroll to the second-last comment.'

As I do, I see that it was posted by Rita, which can't be good for the poor sucker involved.

Haha, guess who, guess what. Does it matter? It does when one social pariah desperately wants

> a date to the formal but the object of her desire
> is already going with his ex. That is, if she is
> his ex ...

Just in case it wasn't obvious enough, she's posted a picture of Shehadie. He's sitting with a group of people at the beach, a cake on the blanket in front of them. He's grinning at a girl with long blonde hair who's smiling back at him. Their hands are intertwined and he looks happy. Happier than I've ever seen him – at work, at school, at the party last night. Happier than he's ever looked when he's with me.

The rest of the day goes by in a blur. I don't remember hanging up the phone with Sue, or logging off my computer. All I remember is shoving my headphones into my ears and listening to depressing Adele love songs which bring on an avalanche of tears. Later, I move from sadness to anger, and so does my music selection – Linkin Park, Taylor Swift and Simple Plan remind me that life is never simple. And neither are people for that matter.

Marie comes in and asks me to listen to her reading homework, and I use all my emotional strength to put on a brave face. When we're done, she kisses my cheek and I pat her on the head. She already has more sass than I do. She'd never let Dad rule her life, or let a boy break her heart.

She must have told Mum that something's up, because minutes later Mum appears with some *yansoon*, a comforting tea that is the Lebanese answer to life's many ailments.

'What's wrong, *hayeti*?' she asks me, brushing my hair away from my face.

She really has made us her entire life. I wonder what she was like at my age.

'*Mareeda*, I think,' I say, 'I must be sick. I feel like I'm going to vomit.'

She moves the garbage bin by my desk closer to me. 'I shouldn't have let you go to that party in the cold,' she says. 'Or so your dad keeps saying.'

I sigh. 'Dad will say anything to avoid me going out.'

'When I was your age, my dad wouldn't let me go make tabouli at my cousin Shereen's house because her brother was home from army camp for the weekend and her parents were dead,' she says, smiling. 'He was afraid that people in the village would talk and no one would marry me because I had spent time in a house with a man.'

'We don't need to live in a village for Dad to think that way about me,' I say. 'Times have changed since you were young. I refuse to believe that I'll be ruining my marriage prospects if I go out with my friends. And I wouldn't want to marry a guy who thought like that anyway.'

'My darling,' she says, 'our community is a village. A big gossipy village, where everything is everyone else's business. Your dad has his reasons for wanting to protect you.'

Yes, but he's protecting me from living my life, I want to say, but instead I roll onto my back and clutch my stomach. Mum looks concerned and I love her for it.

'Get some rest,' she says. 'I've taken the phone off the hook in case you want to sleep.'

'Thanks, Mama,' I say. 'You're the best.'

I spend the rest of the day drifting in and out of sleep, cursing Shehadie for making me feel emotionally and physically sick.

—⟋⟍—

I don't go to school on Monday. I don't have the energy for it. By 10 am, I receive a text from Shehadie.

> Ignore whatever you've seen on Vanessa's FB note.
> Give me a chance to talk to you. There's a lot to
> explain.

I respond with a simple:

> I have nothing to say to you right now

I spend the rest of the day watching re-runs on Foxtel, trying to block everything out of my mind. But I can't, and I'm embarrassed by how often I check my phone. Part of me never wants to see or hear from him again, but a larger part wants him to call me so I can yell at him to my broken heart's content. But he doesn't try to fight for me. He just leaves me alone.

'I can't figure out if that's worse,' I tell Sue when she rings to check up on me.

'I can totally understand you wanting a confrontation,' she says. 'But to be honest, I think you may need to hear him out. He looked really bummed today, like he was carrying the weight of the world on his shoulders.'

'That's not my problem,' I say, hardening myself in preparation for facing him tomorrow. 'You play with fire, you get burnt.'

'Um, okay,' she says.

We chat a bit about homework and then hang up.

By Tuesday, my anger has turned into a far scarier rage and I walk to school with an attitude that says I don't give a damn.

That said, I don't want a confrontation – with liar boys or bitchy girls – so I keep to myself for most of the day. I go to the library at lunchtime for some journal-writing time, but Sue and Nicole track me down and drag me outside to our usual spot.

'I don't want to sit here,' I say, as Nicole dumps my bag on the grass.

'You need some sun. You look scary,' Sue replies. 'Not kidding.'

I glare at her, but feel better once I sit down on the grass with my friends, soaking up the gorgeous weather. I even manage to laugh a few times. Winter is beginning to waste away and a light spring sun hangs in the sky.

'So ...' Jacob says, peering at me, 'Sophie seems to be keeping strong.'

The others nod in agreement as I death-stare him.

'What the hell is that supposed to mean?' I say.

'Well, you were kind of obsessed with him.'

I shove him. 'I was not.'

'Come on, Soph,' Nicole says. 'We were all waiting for it to happen.'

'To happen like this?'

'No, of course not!' she says.

'Well, nothing's going to happen now,' I say, unwrapping my sandwich with such ferocity that they laugh.

'We'll see,' Jacob says. 'Maybe not right now, but I have a feeling the next instalment isn't too far away.'

'What's the girlfriend like, anyway?' Nicole asks. 'Or ex-girlfriend. Or whatever she is. With Vanessa and Rita, you never know what's true and what isn't.'

'Didn't you see the photo?' Sue says. 'Whatever she is, she's blonde and attractive.'

'And probably tall,' I say. 'Just to compound my suffering. Next I'll find out she's a model.'

They smile at me.

'Let's do American teen-movie comparisons,' I say. 'Don't worry, I can handle it.'

'If you're sure,' Sue says, and looks at the others.

'Well, if this were an American teen movie, the blonde girl would be captain of the cheer squad,' Thomas says.

'And who would Sophie be?' Nicole asks.

'Erm, the girl with the glasses and braces and messy hair?' Sue asks, puzzled.

'Sue, I *am* the girl with the glasses and braces and messy hair,' I say. 'And, best of all, a dad who won't even let me go to the mailbox without asking when I'll be back.'

'Don't exaggerate, Sophie,' Jacob says. 'Didn't your mother teach you not to lie?'

'I'm not exaggerating. My sister Angela jokes that I'll meet my future husband in the front yard, get married in the backyard, and move into the shed. That's how much faith she has in the removal of my perma-curfew.'

'The curfew doesn't matter,' Thomas says. 'You wouldn't be invited anywhere anyway.'

'Well, at least I don't go around begging for invites,' I say, swatting at him and missing.

'Sophie might turn out to be the character who brings a gun to school because she's tired of being neglected,' Sue says, teasing me. 'She and that bloody journal of hers would be immortalised.'

I bury my head in my hands. 'Awww, why me?'

'I didn't think our Soph was capable of such a thing,' Thomas says. 'But now ... well, I'm not so sure.'

'You guys are so slack,' I say. 'Seriously, I'm over him and his stupid girlfriend, and his stupid muscly arms and his stupid tan and his stupid smiling eyes. OVER HIM. Time to move on.' I put my hands in my lap to signify that I've made a decision.

'Over him?' Thomas says, cracking up. 'Yeah, right.'

'And here I was thinking you guys were good friends. Silly me,' I say, slapping myself on the forehead.

'Seriously, Soph? You won't be over him in a million years,' Thomas says. 'Come on! You pashed him at a party with complete disregard for the fact that it could get back to your dad. From the moment you did it, you were floating on a cloud, and as soon as you found out there was another chick in the picture you started plotting his death, speaking in tongues and thinking of ways you could get a dead bird into his locker.'

'Tom has a point,' Sue says.

I put down my sandwich, tired of fighting them, of fighting it. 'What's the point, honestly? I wouldn't like someone to steal my boyfriend so why would I do it to her? That's assuming I even stand a chance ...' I start to tear up.

Sue rubs my back. 'Well, for starters, you like him. And secondly, it's not as if he's going out with the girl, he's just taking her to the formal. And before you say anything, I know you were looking forward to going with someone, but for all you know, so was she. And he was probably her high school boyfriend, but he broke up with her because he met you.'

I like the sound of her excuse and wonder if that makes me a bad person.

'I get where you're coming from,' I say. 'But there's too much heartache and drama already. I don't know if I want to go there.' Except, of course, I desperately do.

'Go out with me and make him jealous,' Thomas says.

We all crack up laughing at the suggestion, including Thomas.

'But seriously, Soph,' Sue goes on, 'I know you want to get over it and move on, but I don't see how that's gonna happen. I'm your friend and I love you, but I gotta dish it out. I mean, I can practically see the frisson in the air when you're talking to him.'

'The what?' Jacob asks.

'Sue's been poking fun at Sophie about frizzing something or other for ages now,' Nicole says, shrugging.

Sue laughs. 'The frisson – you know, the thrill, the chemistry. She likes him, he likes her. Problem is, he's scared to do anything about it now, because you've made it clear you want nothing to do with him. And you're prepared to live in the shadow of what could have been, because you're too proud to admit the ex doesn't matter.'

'What is it that you like about him?' Thomas asks, sitting up.

'Nothing anymore,' I say. 'He lied to me. But you know what, it's not like it's a big loss. We were always like this – friendly, then not. Getting on and agreeing about everything, then criticising each other like it's Question Time in Parliament. We've always fought over dumb things.' I continue harping on about it.

'See, even now you can't stop talking about him,' Thomas says.

'At least I can stop talking,' I counter.

'Yeah, not today, you can't,' he replies, elbowing me.

I can't avoid Shehadie forever. I know this because he seeks me out just as much as I seek him out. And even though I don't want to admit it to anyone, myself included, my fragile heart could use an explanation.

He finds me at my locker just after lunch. I'm frantically trying to find my unit of study outline for Business, hoping it will shed some light on what I should be revising for the HSC. The bell has already rung, and yet I can tell he wants to talk.

'Sophie,' he says, drawing out my name in a long breath.

My back is turned to him but I can hear his pain. The scorned woman inside me is overjoyed that I have the power to hurt him, and wants to whip around and yell and scream at him. But the seventeen-year-old girl just wants to know why. I go with the seventeen-year-old girl.

'Why?' I say.

He swallows. 'I don't know.'

'You don't know why you're going out with her? Or you don't know why you lied to me about it? Or you don't know why you kissed me in public knowing there was someone else in the picture? Which of the above questions do you *not know* the answer to?'

'I'm not going out with her, I swear!' he says. 'I swear to God, Soph, it was never like that. I'm not like that.'

I peer at him, trying to let the anger in me win the arm wrestle with the tears.

'Don't swear to God,' I say. 'Especially when I know nothing about your reputation.'

'I can swear to God because I'm not lying,' he says, slinging his backpack over his shoulder. 'And there are aspects of my reputation that I'd rather forget, but when it comes to Jen ... Well, she and I have a long history that's hard to explain.'

I turn my back on him and slam my locker door shut. 'You have a minute,' I say, still facing my locker. 'Explain to me why you kissed me in the middle of the dance floor at a party in front of bitchy, gossipy people. When you know I've never had a boyfriend, let alone kissed anyone, so it might have meant something to me.'

He doesn't say anything. I turn back to face him. There are tears in my eyes. 'Tell me, Shehadie.'

'I didn't know you'd never been kissed.'

'Is that all you can say? I trusted you, you bastard. Don't say you didn't know, because you knew everything. You knew me and my pathetic life and my struggles with my family and the dramas with my friends. You knew it all! That kiss was what I needed to be happy, you stupid, spineless, arrogant arsehole, and now it's ruined like everything else. What kind of person kisses someone when they have a girlfriend?'

'Will you just listen to me, Sophie?' he says, exasperated.

'Don't you dare raise your voice at me!'

'Shut up and let me talk,' he growls, stepping forward and backing me against the lockers, one arm on either side of me. If it wasn't so awful it would be sexy. 'I'm not seeing her. It's been over for ages, and even then it wasn't anything. I've grown up with her.'

'Great,' I say. 'A history. This just keeps getting better and better. Just go away and leave me alone.'

'I didn't do anything wrong! You gotta stop letting those stupid girls make you feel shit about yourself. You're better than that.'

I stare at him through my tears. 'Are you taking her to the formal?' I ask softly, looking away so he doesn't see the hope in my eyes.

'Only because I promised her ages ago. She's taking me to hers too. Not that I really want to go after that football game. It's only because –'

My death stare cuts him off. 'I don't want to talk to you ever again,' I whisper, shoving past him and walking away as fast as I can.

I'm halfway down a flight of stairs when he leans over the rail and yells out to me. 'Come on, Soph, please.'

I ignore him.

'Seriously, what about class?' he says.

'Stuff class,' I say through my tears, and run to the toilets and vomit. Then I sit on the toilet seat for the entire period and cry.

23

I hate it when the truth makes sense

The next week the cops come back to the school to investigate a few leads. It's all we can talk about. In Society and Culture, Mrs Cafree gives up hope of a normal lesson and asks us instead about our uni preferences. She gives me a funny look when I tell her my first choice is accounting at UWS, and I wonder if Dad is the only person on this planet who doesn't know it's totally wrong for me.

'Well, good luck, Sophie,' she says, then does her best to steer the conversation away from the police investigation by telling us how much she's enjoyed the essays we wrote after our debate. I'm surprised when she singles me out, saying I put forward very clever arguments.

My high is cut short when Zayden sniggers at the back of the room.

'What's your problem?' I yell out. 'Seriously?'

'I'm laughing because you just got commended for arguments that probably don't make any sense,' he scoffs.

A few people chuckle, but remarkably I don't care.

'To ignorant people like you, I'm sure,' I respond.

'Wow,' Sue whispers next to me. 'I like the Sophie who speaks up.'

'Whatever,' Zayden says. 'You just keep telling yourself things to make you feel important.'

'You know what, Zayden, I will. You, meanwhile, can continue to act like a thug. I'd suggest making the most of it while you're in high school, because clearly you've already peaked and this is the best it's ever going to get for you. Shame it's practically over, ay?'

'Sophie,' Mrs Cafree warns.

'Sorry, miss, but someone's gotta say it. I reckon everything we think we know now is going to change when we finish school.'

'You're right about that,' she says, smiling. 'And at the risk of sounding like I'm taking sides, which I certainly don't want to do, I must say that your essay made some very interesting observations on stereotypes. If you're interested in that kind of thing you might want to look into taking some social science subjects at uni, or doing an arts degree.'

I nod vaguely.

'What was your essay on, Sophie?' Daniel Sleiman asks as we leave the room.

'Um, I just wrote about how our parents needed to adjust to being here, but that our generation needs to mesh the old and the new together because we're the glue between the two cultures.'

'That's really interesting,' he says. 'Good for you, Sophie.'

—ᴍ—

Later that afternoon, Sister Magdalena walks a group of us down to the school common room, where the police want to show us a few pictures. They're probably afraid that if they do it in a bigger group, we'll all stay quiet.

I feel nervous when I enter the common room, but I don't know why. I doubt that I'll know anyone in the pictures, considering I spend all my spare time inside my house.

One of the police officers, a hottie named Constable Christie, notices my concern and reassures me that they do this all the time and there's nothing to worry about. Of course, he's going to say that – he has no idea what it's like to be a Lebanese girl torn between two worlds.

They show us what seems like hundreds of screen shots and eventually I start to relax. I have no idea who any of these people are.

'Why did it take so long to get to this point?' I ask. 'The brawls were in January.'

'It's a long process,' Constable Christie says. 'We had to tie in what footage we had with witnesses' statements about who was in the street. It was a busy night of celebration, and not everyone who was on the street that night was there to vandalise property.'

'We go through mobile phone records, look at our notes and the footage from traffic cameras, then we speak to witnesses again,' a female officer adds. 'For example, if we identify a car, we'll question the driver, which may lead us to a passenger who knows more. Maybe they remember another car that they parked behind or across from, which had persons of interest in it. Basically, we go down a range of different paths to get to the right one. We're dealing with younger people too, so we need to make sure they're willing to talk, and if they do that they're not lying. We check everything.'

Rita's in our group and chooses that moment to speak up. 'Wait,' she says. 'Go slower, I recognise someone.'

'Okay, think carefully,' Constable Christie says. 'We'll take as long as you need.'

I roll my eyes as Rita starts talking about how she'd seen two boys at a party. I bet she's just trying to impress the cops with how popular she thinks she is. I start to doze off when I hear a gasp from Sister Magdalena behind me.

'Oh, wow,' Rita says. 'That's a boy in our class. His name's Zayden. And look, Sister, there's that Abdo guy from Year Eleven.'

'And Mr Yacoub from Year Ten,' Sister Magdalena says slowly.

On the screen, a group of boys from our school are standing in front of a shop. With them, looking like he'd rather be somewhere else, is a boy I'd know anywhere.

'Can you zoom in?' I say in shock.

The boy is attempting to cover his face with his hoodie, but I recognise all five foot, seven inches of him.

'Who is he?' Constable Christie asks, looking at me.

I can see Rita is about to answer for me. Rita, who's just sentenced an entire group of boys from our school to police questioning. Rita, who has a jubilant look on her face for having gotten me at last. I can't give her the satisfaction of saying it. So when she opens her mouth, I beat her to it.

'That's my brother,' I whisper, and the world comes crashing down around me.

'I don't know why I went,' Andrew says. 'I thought it was stupid. But all these other boys were going and they were all fired up. That Malouf guy sent us all text messages – he said we were insulting our culture if we didn't go, and my friends were all saying he was right. So I just went along with them.'

I feel sick to my stomach as I listen to my brother's excuses for what is probably the dumbest thing he's ever done in his whole life.

Andrew and my parents are in the living room, but I can hear them talking from my spot at the top of the stairs. I peer through the railing and see Dad sitting in an armchair, head bent, hand on his chin, his index finger and thumb resting on either cheek. He looks as if he's trying to hold his mouth closed when it very much wants to yell about the latest failure of his family. He's been sitting in the same spot for hours, ever since he found out that Andrew had bowed to peer pressure and become a vigilante for a cause he had no idea about. I'm glad Sister Magdalena called with a warning before the cops arrived, otherwise they may have gotten here only to see Dad kill his only son with his bare hands.

'I honestly wasn't thinking,' Andrew says. 'I just wanted to do something. They made me feel as though our family was being attacked.'

'Oh, this is not about your family, you stupid boy!' Dad yells, rising from his seat. 'This is about you and your stupid decision-making. Your failure to think things through. Your inability to see past your own selfishness. Where was your brain that night, Andrew? Didn't you think of the consequences? Couldn't you have stopped for one moment to contemplate how your mother would have felt if something had happened to you? What if you had hurt somebody and had to go to prison?'

'I wouldn't have gone to prison, I'm not old enough –'

'But you are old enough to know right from wrong! Even Marie is old enough to know, and she would have made a better decision than you. People were injured that night. People were attacked while going about their everyday business. How would you have felt if someone had attacked me while I was taking out the garbage, would you have liked it?'

'No! But we were trying to prevent that from happening in the first place. The mob –'

'The mob was you, Andrew,' Mum says quietly. She's sitting opposite Dad, next to the son they both thought could do no wrong. 'All of you young boys, barely hatched out of your eggs. The country was outraged at those men in Cronulla – drunk, disorderly, uneducated. And then you and your silly friends had to go and be exactly like them, and worse. What did you achieve, you silly boy? You lost sight of everything we raised you to believe! How many times have we taught you to be like our Lord in a confrontation? If you had turned your other cheek that night, Andrew, this would not have happened.'

'Oh, what did I do, Lord, to deserve such punishments?' Dad wails. 'Is this a penance for some great sin? Why the constant shame upon my family? My sister, her boyfriend and a *mseebi* we got rid of years ago. A son who thinks it is okay to be a warrior fighting for a stupid situation he knows nothing about. A daughter who does a disservice to her family and her community by airing their dirty laundry instead of protecting them and being the silent woman she ought to be. *Laysh hal aybie ya Rub?*'

I don't know how, but suddenly I'm standing in the living room too. 'Why a shame of this magnitude, Dad? I can't believe you don't know. Stop acting like you're so innocent in all of this.'

Dad glares angrily at me, and Mum gasps loudly. Even Andrew – sullen, proud and arrogant all at the same time – looks shocked; he stares at me with his mouth gaping open.

'Half of this is your fault,' I say. 'Do you ever prevent Andrew from going anywhere? Do you ask him a hundred questions before he goes out to a party, or wait for him until he gets home to see if he was lying to you? Do you tell him that no one will marry him if he asks to go out for coffee with his friends at night? No. Just because he's a boy, he's allowed to do whatever he wants. Because he's almost a man, no one can interfere in his business. You've never butted into his life or told him he couldn't work, or have fun, or made him study subjects that you think are suitable.

'You're so busy disciplining me and the girls, and complaining about Leila and her Asian fiancé and her stupid tattoo, that your son thinks he can do whatever he wants in life without any consequences. Just because he's a man. Well, that's not how things are in the world, Dad. As you can see, that attitude has finally caught up with him.'

'*Wli*, Sophie!' Dad says. 'How dare you!'

But the words are tumbling out of my mouth before I have a chance to process them in my brain.

'And don't tell me I'm doing a disservice to our family and community. For the zillionth time, I was just a witness. Not that it matters anyway, because anyone who breaks the law or does something terrible deserves to be punished. It's the way of the world. You wouldn't be accusing me of doing a disservice to my community if Andrew had done the right thing.'

Dad is silent, his face red, his eyes bloodshot. Mum sits on the corner of the couch, weeping, breaking my heart. Dad is about to speak, totally enraged, when Andrew cuts in.

'She only thinks like that because of her Aussie boyfriend,' he blurts out. 'She was never like this before, only since she started seeing him.'

The whole house is quiet. Dad looks at me like he doesn't know who I am anymore.

'I'm not going out with an Aussie guy, you idiot,' I say to Andrew. 'He's my friend, he's in my class and he's half-Lebanese. His name is Shehadie, and he probably knows more Lebanese words than Leila. Plus, he actually knows how to spell the name of his mum's village. Don't you dare act high and mighty, because the stupid boys that you hang out with have made him feel like shit since he arrived at our school. He took it like a true Christian, like a man, which is something you could learn from him.'

Dad points his finger at us. 'Shame on both of you!' he yells. 'Get out of my sight! I don't want to look at either of you.'

'Fine,' we yell at the same time.

But where Andrew runs up the stairs to his room, I run out of the house and into the pouring rain. I can't believe what's just happened.

I see Viola's bike in the front yard and grab it and hop on, pedalling as fast as I can, far away from all my problems. My Aunty Leila and her wild ways. My crush and the girl he can't leave behind. My mum and her passiveness. My dad and his ignorance. Everyone's ignorance.

I ride without knowing where I'm going. The rain pours down and drenches me, and I pray that it will wash away every negative thing I'm feeling because I'm sick of fighting a tide that's always dragging me under.

24

I hate that the answer to a problem is usually the one you don't want to hear

The tears streaming down my face feel almost as heavy as the pouring rain. I'm pedalling so fast I can barely see where I'm going and almost collide with a pedestrian. I stop and realise I'm in Shehadie's street. He's the only person I want to see right now so it's no coincidence I've ended up here.

I chuck Viola's bike on his front lawn and bang on the door, forgetting this is the home of an elderly couple. He answers, wearing a white T-shirt and jeans. Even though he's got glasses on and is holding study notes, he looks so hot I almost forget why I'm here.

'Sophie?' he says. 'What's going on?'

He looks puzzled, but still pulls me off the doorstep and into the shelter of the veranda. I blubber something incoherent.

'You're soaking wet!' he says. 'Did you walk here? Never mind, we can talk about that later. Come into the living room and I'll get you some towels. Silly duffer.'

I smile inwardly at this boy who can sound like an Australian grandmother one minute and a bloke's bloke the next.

He makes me a cup of tea, and then I find myself sitting on a rug in his grandmother's house and pouring out my heart to the person I swore I'd never talk to again. We talk about everything – exams and Dora and Leila and Andrew and the police and my dad. And somewhere in the middle of all that, when my heart stops sinking from the weight of all my dramas and I go quiet, he hugs me.

After what seems like a long while, I pull away.

'I'm an idiot,' I whisper. 'I'm so sorry for how I treated you. How the hell were you supposed to know I was banking on a date to the formal?'

'It's okay,' he says, smiling at me. 'I know how necessary melodrama is to your sense of being. If overreacting meant that much to you, I guess I was happy to be part of it. There's no way you can go into accounting without a dose of the theatrical to keep you afloat.'

'I was a little jealous,' I admit. 'I was hoping that this year everything would change. And by everything I mean I'd look hot at the formal and have a gorgeous date as my arm candy. And I'm only half-joking about that being everything, which makes me sound shallow, I know.'

'The thing is, you never let me explain why I'm going with Jen.'

'Because I really didn't want to know. And I still don't.'

'Well, you need to, especially if things are going to go further between us. She's a part of my life and I don't want to change that.'

I stare at him in shock, wondering how I get roped into these situations. Does the guy want to go out with me, but still have his girlfriend on the side?

'Jen's mum and my mum were best friends,' he says. 'Jen's in eighty per cent of my childhood pictures. Our mums used to take us everywhere together, and from the moment we got to high school they kept saying how much they wanted us to go to the formal together. They couldn't wait to see how great we'd look in the pictures. So going with Jen is my way of doing something for my mum, that's all.'

I nod.

'You're disappointed,' he says.

'No, not at all.'

'I can tell you are. Don't be embarrassed. Girls get hung up on that crap. God knows why.'

I shrug. 'There's a lot invested in it. We look forward to it for a long time, and keep the pictures even longer. And maybe it's more than that for me, seeing as I've never really gone on a date or anything. It's like a semi-date.'

'Please don't make me feel guilty,' he says.

'It's not my intention, I swear to you.'

He sighs. 'I believe you. Aaah, this whole situation just sucks. Never in a million years did I think that my mum would die, I'd get expelled from school and my dad would be too wrapped up in his own grief to deal with me. Or that I'd move in with my grandparents, go to a Lebanese school and actually meet someone I like there. Someone I like a lot.' He smiles at me. 'But since we're talking like this, I should probably tell you –'

'Oh God,' I say. 'What now? I'm not sure I can take any more.'

He laughs. 'I'm serious, Soph. I don't want you to find this stuff out from someone else. There's more to why I moved here ... or was moved, I should say. I got expelled from my last school. After Mum died, I just started hating everything. I felt so hurt, and so alone. I did everything I could to escape the hurt ... including drugs –'

I gasp and he smiles at me apologetically.

'Nothing hard,' he says, looking ashamed. 'But enough to do some damage to my reputation, my relationships and my record. I got myself into some pretty bad situations, even with my dad.'

'How bad are we talking?' I ask.

'Some pot in my room, passing out in the bathtub, waking up and going to school. Mostly it was just about forgetting everything. But then it started messing with my head. Dad was working hard to avoid coming home to his wifeless house, and I got convinced he was having an affair with his secretary.'

'Oh God, Shehadie, that is so clichéd,' I say, not sure whether to laugh or hug him.

'And that's only the half of it. One time, I saw them together and he laughed at one of her jokes. It killed me because it was the first time he'd been happy in months. I was gutted. I grabbed the first thing I could and threw it at her car, breaking the windscreen. She resigned from her job, even though she'd been working for Dad for ages. She was just so shaken up. That was the straw that broke the camel's back. I was shipped to Tayta and Pop's place, and then I met you and suddenly the darkest period of my life feels like it happened for a reason ...'

My face goes red.

'I hope it goes to show you, Soph, that you're not the only one with dramas and problems. We're all teenagers, and we're all human. We just have different issues, and we all deal with them differently. You write about yours in your journal – which I hope will convince you that it'll be a waste if you don't study arts or something other than accounting.'

'Everyone needs to lay off me and my journal,' I say, shoving him.

He laughs and then looks at me seriously. 'I should've told you earlier about Jen, but I was a bit of a coward. I wanted to tell you about the other stuff too, especially because you might have heard about it at the footy game, but I was too embarrassed. It didn't bother me before, maybe because it felt like a typical teenage phase, but then I freaked out that it might change things between us. I would've loved to go with you to the formal, but maybe hot Sophie could spare me a dance?'

He searches my face for an answer, then starts smiling because he knows it before I say anything.

'Um, have we met?' I say. 'Need I remind you of my unbelievable awkwardness that will guarantee I have a lot of dances to spare?'

'You don't give yourself enough credit,' he says, reaching for my hand. 'You looked so good at that cruise thing. And not just because you were in a miniskirt.'

I don't know what to say, so I comment on his glasses.

'I wore them the first few days of school, remember?'

'Don't flatter yourself, Goldsmith,' I say, giggling.

'I don't need to flatter myself. I remember you checking me out.'

'You remind me of Clark Kent,' I say suddenly.

'What, my glasses?'

'Everything. Your look, your mannerisms, your attitude ...'

'So is that a good thing or a bad thing?'

'It's a very good thing,' I say, smiling.

'Because Clark Kent is Superman?' he asks coyly.

I grin. 'Something like that. I have a bit of a superhero thing.'

He holds out his hand to pull me up, and we walk back down the corridor. On the way, I notice a poster on one of the doors.

'Is this your room?' I ask, peering around the door.

'Yes, but you're not going to like what's in there.'

I open the door wide and walk inside. It's a typical teenage boy's room: TV and stereo, video games and DVDs strewn about, and lots and lots of boxes. There's a suitcase in the corner, piled high with winter clothes. On top of the pile is Shehadie's bulldog jumper.

I turn to face him. 'Are you going away?'

'Something like that,' he says, shuffling his foot. 'Dad and I are going to rekindle the bromance by doing everything Mum wished she'd done before she died. We're going to have fun in Disneyland, ski in Aspen, shop up a storm in New York, get our French on in New Orleans and get drenched at Niagara Falls. And then we're going to eat gelato in Rome, do the *Sound of Music* tour in Salzburg, visit the Tower of London and the Mona Lisa, along with all this other stuff.'

I smile at him. 'So it's like a gap year?'

He nods. 'All five months of it.'

'What? Five months?' I say, shocked. 'When? What about exams? Uni? Your life?'

What about me? I want to ask.

'By the time I leave, the exams will be done and dusted. Everything else just goes on hold. Plus it'll give me more time to think about what I want to do at uni. I'm thinking psychology, because I've had a lot of practice on you.'

I slap his arm. 'Sue wants to go to the States. Maybe you guys can meet up?'

'Maybe,' he says noncommittally.

I'm quiet.

'Don't you have anything to say?' he asks.

'How long have you known?' I ask softly, testing the waters.

I wonder if he'd thought my heart was unbreakable, but then I remember telling him I never wanted to speak to him again. After that performance, my heart would have been the last thing on his mind.

'We booked three days ago,' he replies. 'It seemed right at the time. I mean, school would be finished, you never wanted to speak to me again, and I know Zayden and I will email every other day so that particular friendship won't be affected.'

We both laugh.

'At least he's been a bit better to you lately,' I point out. 'Then again, was he going to be mean to you forever?'

He smiles, then looks pensive. 'I have to go, Soph, for her sake,' he says, staring at the suitcase. 'She was the most amazing woman. And I owe it to Dad too, because he knows he stuffed up big with me. But who knows, I might be back before you know it, before you've even had a chance to realise that accounting isn't for you and enrolled in something else.'

'Maybe by that time my dad will let me speak to boys,' I say.

We stare at each other for a while.

'So, when are you leaving?' I finally ask.

'One week after the formal. So there's plenty of time for some final hurrahs.'

'I don't hurrah,' I say. 'Especially if I don't know what's going to happen.'

'I really am sorry, Soph. But let's just play it by ear.'

'You say that now, but when you're travelling through America wearing that horrendous jumper and thinking you're like Superman because I stupidly told you you were, and there are gorgeous women everywhere, willing to fall at your feet or in your bed, I'll be the last thing on your mind.'

'I doubt it,' he says.

I don't reply, because I want to believe him.

'I'd better get home and face the music,' I say, after another silence that seems to last a decade. 'Dad's probably going berserk.'

'You didn't tell him where you were going? Wow, you really are breaking the rules.' He suddenly looks paranoid. 'He's not going to come looking for you here, is he? You didn't write my name in that bloody journal of yours and leave it lying around?'

'What did I say about flattering yourself?'

'Sorry, miss,' he says. 'I'll text Sue to come and get you so you don't have to ride in the rain. I hope her boot fits that bike.' He peers through the window. 'It's so little – is it even yours?'

—◦—

When Sue rings the bell and I open the front door with red-rimmed eyes, she doesn't know what to make of the situation. She glances from me to Shehadie and then back to me again, and says, 'I'll ask questions later.' I love her for knowing that I'll tell her everything in my own time.

It's stopped raining, but there are still some clouds in the sky. I think of Shehadie leaving and wonder when I'll get my rainbow. Sue backs the car into the driveway and opens the boot. Shehadie lifts the bike effortlessly and puts it inside.

'Is there anything you can't do?' I tease.

'I pretty much suck at flying,' he says with a smirk.

'Shame, I could have used some visits from overseas. Europe is awfully far away.'

'We'll work something out,' he says, wiping my hair away from my face. 'Now go on home and face your dad.'

'Shehadie, I'm sorry, but I really have to know. What the hell is with that ugly bulldog jumper?'

He laughs. 'It's the Yale University mascot. Dad studied there on exchange in the eighties, and that jumper was my mum's favourite.'

I smile at him as I get into Sue's car. Finally, a reasonable explanation for his terrible flaw. The only problem? Now I think he's perfect.

25

I hate discovering that my loved ones are hiding the biggest secrets

By the time Sue drops me home, it's getting dark. Mum is perched on a chair on the veranda waiting for me.

'Thank God,' she exclaims as I walk up the front path. 'I was worried sick about you.'

I go to say something but she waves her hand at me. 'It doesn't matter now. Well, not to me anyway. I didn't think you were doing anything wrong.'

She gets up and grabs me in a hug.

'I wish you'd stood up for me,' I whisper to her.

She pulls away and looks at me. 'Is that what you think? That I never stand up for you?'

I don't say anything and Mum sinks back into her chair.

'I stand up for you in my own ways, Sophie,' she says. 'You know in our culture it is wrong for a woman to raise her voice like a man. She has to behave like a lady.'

'And I think that, along with a lot of other cultural rules, is bullshit,' I say, sitting down on the top step.

'It's not the same for every village,' she says. 'Ours was just a bit more old-fashioned than others. But don't worry, we Lebanese women have our ways when it comes to the men in our lives. How do you think I got your dad to shut up when you were yelling at him? Just one look from me and he knew he had to let you say your piece, which I don't exactly blame you for. And don't let me get started on that party you went to recently ...'

She gives me a knowing look.

'I hate how the girls are treated so differently,' I say finally. 'It's ridiculously unfair. And that stupid rule about no one marrying you because you go out or sleep somewhere away from home is crap. Everyone does it these days. Am I never going to be able to spend the night at a hotel or sleepover for a friend's birthday?'

'That's a rule I agree with, for now,' she says. 'It is for your own safety. But we'll cross that bridge when we get to it. I know you worry, Sophie, but you're still young. Don't be in a rush to grow up so fast, okay? Take it from me, once you're too old, you're too old.'

She smiles gently at me and I smile back.

'When you're older, you can run your house differently,' she says. 'You won't have to do all the housework, your daughter won't have separate rules to her brother, you can go out with your friends without being labelled a bad mother.'

I love how Mum's teaching me a lesson without even trying. Here I am thinking I'm invisible, when she's missed out on so much. My heart aches as I realise she's never really had a chance to be young.

'Your father and I are from a different time *and* a different place,' she says, 'which makes it harder for us than for parents who were raised here. We think of things so differently.

What we're trying to do is meet you guys in the middle, but both journeys will take a while to reach their destination.

'I want you to know, Sophie, I'm not as powerless as you might think. It is good for a man to feel like he is the boss. I know how to negotiate with your father and make him think that my ideas are his ideas. It's certainly better than screaming the roof down around us.'

I smile at this side of Mum I've never seen before.

'You are old enough to know this now, and you'll see it for yourself soon enough. Men run around like headless chooks without us. So don't feel sorry for me, okay?'

She gets up from her chair and pulls me up off the floor. 'Go up to your room,' she says, patting me on the back. 'I'll send your father up in a few minutes.'

'Do I have to?' I ask in a singsong voice.

'If you want to stop feeling invisible in this house, yes.' She takes a look at my face and smiles mischievously. 'Don't think I don't know what goes on inside my own home,' she says, winking.

———∭———

I walk inside, and head upstairs quietly. When I pass Andrew's room, I notice the door's closed, surprise, surprise.

'He is grounded for a month and not very happy about it,' Dad says behind me. 'I think the police will be laying charges – they arrested that Zayden boy. But as Sister Magdalena told me, Andrew's involvement was minimal so he will probably get a community service sentence.'

I spin around. 'Baba,' I start, but he waves me into my room.

'We'll talk inside, Sophie.'

I sit on my desk chair, and he sits on the bed. He looks like he's struggling to know how to begin.

'You were right today, Sophie,' he says finally. 'Everything you said, you had a point.'

I open my mouth, but he puts his hand up, signalling that he needs to finish.

'I didn't like the manner in which you said it, especially in front of your siblings – raising your voice at me like that. But I am willing to think that's because you thought you didn't have any other way to talk to me, which you probably didn't. Unfortunately, Sophie, we don't live in a perfect world. Your mother and I were raised in a very simple environment. Things were different. A girl lived with her parents, spent some time in the village with her friends, got married and started a new life. There was hardly any work except sewing or being a housemaid, so everything was far simpler.

'Our people, they love to talk. It is intrinsic – is that how you say? – to their nature. They can't help it. We also pride ourselves on the strength of a family, which means the people within that family need to be decent and solid. To us, that means a woman should not have many boyfriends or live outside the home. If she does, she is not going to commit as well as she should to her husband and children. Your generation may think differently, but we can't escape what our generation thinks.

'One day, you will be all grown-up and you will meet a man and fall in love. He might be from a different village, so his parents won't know what a great catch you are. How you're a good girl who respects her parents, goes to church, has housewife skills. All the things we Lebanese people love.

His opinion won't always matter, but theirs will, so we want to make sure that they have nothing bad to say about you or us.'

'People are always going to talk, Dad,' I say, rolling my eyes. 'Does that mean I have to stop living my life? It's not fair that I'm not allowed to enjoy myself just in case others decide to gossip.'

'Life is unfair, Sophie. You think I am a monster dictator because I never let you go anywhere. I also think you know I had a fight with your Aunty Leila and she has not been to our house since. This was something I didn't want you to know about ever if I could prevent it, but the truth always has a way of coming out from the shadows.

'When your aunty was around your age, we had been in this country about three years. She had adjusted well. She went to a girls' public high school in Lakemba, had plenty of friends, not all Lebanese, and loved to go shopping with them. My mother was always worried about her reputation, but my father, God rest both their souls, could never say no to his beautiful girl. She could have everything she wanted when she smiled.

'When she was in Year Twelve, she met an Australian boy at a party. He was the neighbour of a classmate, three years older than her, and a mechanic. She was in love with him, but told none of us about it. She was right – we would have never understood. Back in those days, mixed marriages were not an option, but to Leila, growing up in that Australian school, none of her parents' old rules mattered. After school, she would meet him in parks, at train stations, in the shops. Anywhere to see him. A few months into the relationship, he wanted to take things … how shall I say this … further. To cut a long story short, he forced himself on her.'

I gasp in horror.

'She fell pregnant, and she never saw him again. He went travelling and we never heard from him after that. The worst part of it was that she trusted him and the friend that introduced them, and because she did, her life was ruined.'

'That's got nothing to do with where she went to school, Dad,' I point out. 'Or who she hung out with, even. Girls at my school are very liberal too. Not everyone sticks to the old ways, you know.'

'No, I guess not,' he says.

'So is this the *mseebi*, the drama, that you and she were fighting about?' I ask. 'Why bring it back up now, after all these years?'

'Because she has gone looking for the child,' he says softly. 'It is not that I don't want her to find it … him or her, I am just afraid that it might open old wounds for her. It was terrible for her to give up the baby, but that boy ruined her life.'

'So, is that why you don't like me hanging around with people you don't know?'

'Partly,' he says. 'It makes things more complicated. We are from a very tight-knit community – we know people, we can ask about them. We can ask someone if they know the family or the village. We can uncover with one phone call what a police detective tries to find out in a year.'

I scoff. 'Dad, this isn't about boys. It's about everything in my life that I feel I don't have a say in. I need a chance to live – it's the only way I'm going to learn.'

But he doesn't let me finish. 'I don't want you to grow up, Sophia. Because when you do, I will stop mattering.'

My eyes fill with tears. It's the most honest exchange I've ever had with my dad.

'You'll always matter to me, Bayyi,' I say. 'But you don't want me going through life like an idiot who avoids things because she's scared.'

'You are right, my darling,' he says, patting my head as he stands up. 'If only I had invested more time in disciplining your brother. It will be a nightmare to start now.'

I smile at him.

'Don't say anything,' he warns me with a half-smile. 'I hope to God you are never right again. For my sake too, you know.'

'Sure, Dad,' I say, laughing and hitting him playfully on the arm.

When he opens the door to walk out of my room, I see Mum standing in the hallway dusting the picture frames on the wall. No wonder these old Lebs know everything. They are so bloody nosey!

26

I hate that sometimes other people's experiences make me understand Dad's reasons for wanting to censor my own

After six years of hearing about how it's the pinnacle of our high school education, the HSC creeps up on us faster than we expect, and before long we're all stressing about it. Despite older friends and family telling us that it isn't the 'be all and end all', there are tears, freak-outs, drama-filled study sessions and phone calls at all hours of the night.

I spend a lot of time in the local library, which offers a break from my loud home and its constant stream of visitors. Occasionally Nicole, Thomas and even Shehadie join me so we can test one another on our study material.

I appreciate Shehadie's efforts to help me, but he's so distracting.

'I'm not joking, Shehadie,' I say, as he throws another paper plane at me. 'You might ace exams without having to study, but unfortunately I'm not as smart as you. I actually have to study if I want to pass.'

'You'll pass,' he says. 'You've got the hottest tutor around.'

'Yeah, that's great,' I reply, laughing. 'But if this mock essay question were in the actual exam, I wouldn't have the vaguest idea how to even start answering it … and my hot tutor won't be around for long either. He's going all over the world, remember?'

'So if I wasn't going to travel you'd go out with me?'

'Maybe. Yes. Oh, I dunno,' I say, exasperated. 'I really need to focus on my notes right now.'

'You're worried I might cheat on you while I'm away?'

I sigh and bite my lip. 'I'm worried I don't stand a chance next to the girls you'll inevitably meet.'

'You're an idiot,' he says, eyeing me intently.

'Am I?'

'You know how I feel about you. How many more ways can I show you? When are you going to be confident enough to accept that someone might choose you over all the other girls in the world?'

I don't know what to say. This is too big a conversation to be having when I'm trying to study for a subject I'm convinced I'm going to fail. But my silence just gives him more room to work on me.

'You're the game-changer, Sophie,' he says, grabbing my hand. 'I can't promise you the rest of my life, because I'm eighteen years old and the rest of my life seems like an eternity away. But I can promise you my youth. To most people I know, that's the most important and exciting thing.'

'We'd never work out,' I argue.

'You're thinking like your dad,' he says after a moment. 'You've bitched constantly about him not giving you a chance to be yourself because he's worried about the consequences, and now you're doing the same thing.'

'You're right,' I sigh, 'but you're going away.'

'What do you want me to say?' he asks testily. 'That I won't go? That I'll give up a chance to fix my broken relationship with Dad so you can be sure that I'm worth fighting for? Because at the moment it seems like you're the one who doesn't want it to work.'

I start to say something, but he keeps going.

'I'm trying to tell you that you matter more to me than any potential holiday fling; that you matter to me more than my pride, which, by the way, is already bruised by your rejection. Think about it from my perspective – I'm pursuing a girl who's like a brick wall, and while I'm away she's probably going to meet some cocky Bruce Wayne type at uni and forget all about Clark Kent halfway across the world.'

And then my walls come down.

'I couldn't find anyone better than Clark Kent,' I admit. 'But you know, Shehadie, you can't blame me for wanting you to fight for me. It's good for my self-esteem to hear all those things. All you've done so far is pash me at a party and pay me some attention, but we've never actually discussed a relationship.'

'So you did this on purpose?' he asks, poking me. 'You women are all the same.'

And then he smiles at me and I smile back, and just like that it feels like everything's going to be okay.

As soon as Leila opens the door, she knows why I'm there.

'He told you,' she says.

'Yes, but whatever came out of Dictator Dad's mouth might have been censored,' I say, rolling my eyes.

'That's true,' she says, smiling. 'I was wondering when you'd come.'

'Well, this isn't exactly a phone-worthy conversation, is it?'

'No, I guess not,' she says, leading me to the kitchen. 'Tea?'

'Milo, thanks.'

'Ah yes, how could I forget? Although isn't Milo a bit childish for someone who's dying to be a grown-up?'

'I'm still legally a child,' I point out.

'For a few more weeks yet, missy.'

'Are you going to start acting like a parent now that you are one?'

She shoots me a look and whacks me across the back of the head.

'Sorry, crossed the line,' I say.

She laughs. 'And I'll do that again if I need to.'

We take our drinks out to her back veranda.

'So,' I say, almost shyly, 'you have a child.'

'A daughter,' she replies, nodding. 'Her name's Dani. Wouldn't have been my choice of name, but she sounds nice on the phone, and her name's not her fault. It's not even short for Danielle, it's just Dani. I can't believe she's your age, just a little bit older. Doesn't seem that long ago that she was born.'

'Isn't it confronting?' I ask. 'Making plans to meet a child who was the result of rape?'

'It's more confronting living a lie, Sophie.'

I look at her quizzically, and she sighs and leans forward in her chair.

'I wasn't raped,' she says. 'There was nothing violent about it. It was … just love, really. Young, silly, thoughtless love, but love nonetheless.'

'Are you for real?' I ask, incredulous.

She nods. 'His name was Callum. I liked him, he liked me. I loved that he was musical, that he had a hot car, that he had long, grungy hair –'

'Ewww.'

'It was the early nineties,' she says. 'He was in a band.'

I make a face at her but she keeps going.

'I spent every chance I could with him. And one day, I wanted more. I just wasn't smart enough to think it through.'

'So you're telling me that my dad's been harbouring a grudge against a guy you willingly slept with? Isn't that a little unfair?'

'Don't look at me like that, Sophie. My mother made up that lie to prevent your dad breaking Callum's kneecaps.'

'He's not that kind of Leb, Leila,' I say, sighing.

'Are you taking his side now?'

'It's not about taking sides. It's about the truth and what's right, don't you think?'

She's silent for a moment.

'Look, I stuffed up, and I did what I could to save myself,' she says finally. 'The funny thing is, it felt wrong to me even then, but I think I would have done anything to keep him. I knew that when he went overseas, it would be the end. In hindsight, it did a lot of damage to me mentally – getting engaged to someone else so I'd have an excuse to have the baby, giving her up, breaking off the engagement, running away ...'

'So you made one regrettable decision and screwed up your life in the process?' I say cynically. This is all starting to sound way too familiar.

'It sounds stupid, but in hindsight, I think that's what it was,' Leila says. 'I just wasn't ready like I thought I was, and I spent years trying to fill a void of my own making.'

'Wow,' I say, looking at her. 'Is that why you've been distant lately?'

'Yeah. It's been a long journey for me to get to this point. And to convince your dad that it's the right thing for me – which of course I didn't manage. But I can't go on not knowing her ...'

'How do you think she feels about it?'

She shrugs. 'She seems pretty open to it. There are processes, you know. She waited till she was old enough ... And her adoptive parents told her when she was young, so it's not like it was a massive shock for her. She didn't come looking for me as an act of rebellion.'

'You're the rebel,' I say, laughing. 'The rebel aunty.'

'The experience *made* me a rebel, Soph,' she says. 'I was just a kid like you when it happened. I didn't think about what I was doing, I just thought of the boy and made a rash decision. And then afterwards, I had to think about finding a solution that wouldn't shame me, because that's how we lived.'

'And continue to live,' I say.

'Yeah,' she says, smiling. 'When I was pregnant and alone, I went through a phase where I understood it – why they want you to wait until marriage. But then afterwards, I went completely the other way. I hated how everyone knew everyone else's business. It was because of other people's opinions that I couldn't keep my baby.'

After a moment, I say, 'It's because of other people's opinions that I avoided an amazing guy for a long time. And now he's about to go overseas and I won't get to spend any more time with him.'

'The half-Anglo kid? I knew you liked him.'

I make a face. 'I think a lot of people knew before I did.'

'So he's going overseas, huh?'

'Yep ... where he'll no doubt meet countless girls who come with a lot less emotional and cultural baggage.'

'Pfft,' she says. 'Beautiful, but boring. So what?'

I give her a sad little smile.

'If it's meant to be, kiddo, it will be,' she says, patting my hair. 'If you let yourself pine, it'll eat away at you. Take it from me. Now's the time to work on yourself.'

I look at her curiously.

'Sophie, you're about to taste social freedom for the first time in seventeen years. Soak it up. Work on your goals. Take the time to build the life you want for yourself based on your interests, your passions, what you read and think and believe. Not the life that your parents or teachers or friends want for you. And when he comes back, if you still want each other, it'll happen.'

'Is this another lesson from your past?' I ask cheekily.

'Kind of,' she says, smirking. 'I've learnt so many lessons, I could go on forever.'

27

I hate banking my entire future on the smallest thing

The smallest thing is a nightmare to write: an entrance essay that's part of my application to study arts and social sciences at the University of Notre Dame. I try to focus on the writing, not on how Dad will react when I tell him what I've done; not on whether personal applications are actually worth anything (the University of Notre Dame doesn't process applications through UAC); and certainly not on the distracting mess in my post-HSC bedroom. I really ought to burn all my study notes, at least for ceremonial purposes.

I stare at the question before me.

> Write a personal essay between 1000 and 1500 words
> that discusses something from your everyday life: e.g.
> food, school, work, family. Relate your selected topic to
> a broader social topic that you think is relevant in society,
> culture or education today.

Thinking about what to write is driving me crazy.

I text Sue: Can't do this. Brain refuses 2 cooperate.

She replies: Then work with your heart ;P

Smart-arse, I scoff, clambering off my bed and back into the chair facing my computer screen. It's no use fighting it, I tell myself. And so I start writing.

Food for Thought

My life can best be described as one big barbecue, the kind that's busy and bubbling with excitement, starring an array of family and friends who filter in and out to enjoy the buffet and move on, or maybe stay for dessert. Like every meal, it represents a delicate fusion of tastes, ideals and characters that make it genuinely exciting. There's always an issue or dilemma to deal with, a little bit of drama and gossip, and generally a great party.

My barbecue fuses together location and background. Location, because the barbecue is quintessentially Australian, and background, because there's nothing more important to the Lebanese than a family meal. Our family barbecue features sausages and steaks next to kafta and marinated meats, tabouli next to garden salad. Our garlic bread isn't the watered-down version with garlic butter smeared on a French baguette. Instead it's pure garlic sandwiched between two large pieces of Lebanese bread, which kind of explains why you can't kiss a Lebanese person after dinner.

Like the food on my table, I'm a cultural dichotomy. I don't know who I am. My father drinks VB and calls his friends 'mate', but encourages me to learn Arabic and read up on the country that he reluctantly left behind. My mother teaches me the secrets and rules of a young girl living in the 'old country', in the hope I will grow up protected from the Western practices that captivate my friends. I'm growing up in a time when men and women have equal opportunities, but my home life doesn't reflect this. There are gender imbalances that are made even more confusing by the fact that my parents have invested so much time and energy in helping me recognise the value of my education.

As a result, even the most enjoyable cultural celebrations leave me feeling isolated. I feel like the garlic sandwiched between two different slices of bread, and I like both slices very much. I don't want to have to choose a side, and even if I could, the other side would question why I was turning away from it.

So on the days we have guests over I sit at the table, away from everyone, eat quickly and make an inconspicuous exit. I go to my room and contemplate my identity. Am I Australian Lebanese or Lebanese Australian?

The Lebanese people I'm surrounded by are not exactly open people; they stick to what they know. If they don't know you, or your parents, or your culture, then you generally don't cut it. I feel like I don't cut it, because I don't know who I am. I don't fit in among the Aussies either. First of all, I have a woggy surname, complete with matching nose. Secondly, how am I supposed to get to know my Aussie friends properly if I'm not allowed to hang out with them? After all, a Lebanese girl isn't supposed to leave the house at night. My ancestors would roll in their graves! What would the village folk say? How could I snag myself a Lebanese husband?

I cherish my blood, but the further I mentally venture away from the little square my parents have fashioned for me, the more my blood thins. I feel like I'm dishonouring my cultural background simply by disagreeing with a few of its norms.

But getting to this point has made me realise just how much I don't want to let my culture go. Despite the fact that I'll probably never return to the country of my ancestors, I finally understand the beauty of the mixed barbecue.

My parents made a long, tumultuous journey here. When they arrived, they started from scratch and built their lives anew, like thousands of migrants before them. Their table – and to some extent, mine – is set with experience, hardship, accomplishment and pride. It's a table that stands strong despite the struggles it has endured; a table that is testament to the 'fair go' this great nation offers.

Despite my confusion over whether to forget my ancestry and embrace my new life, waving the banner of the Southern Cross while humming 'Waltzing Matilda', I know that I'm part of a nation that keeps the dream of a second chance alive.

And should I stray from my roots, there's something other than my blood that will always bring me back. It's that spectacular smell of Lebanese cooking wafting before my woggy nose. And the fact that no matter where I go, there will be a relative waiting to welcome me with open arms. So I'll follow the smell and find my way to the noisiest house on the street, where the men are drinking beer around the barbie and the women are gossiping while preparing lunch. Out front, the kids will be yelling in a mix of English and Arabic while they kick around a football.

And at the table, I'll defiantly claim that I'm Australian by birth, loyal to the land that has fed me, clothed me and educated me. A land that has given me the opportunity to sandwich myself between my two great loves, making me enriched, open-minded and appreciative of my blessings.

I'll look around at the people who have gathered in celebration of everything they've gained and with everyone they love. I'll fill my plate from the feast before me, ready to join the party.

This brings with it a comforting revelation. Australia will always be my home. But every time there's a barbecue, I'll be there, enjoying my culture – on a stick, on a plate, or on some bread. The fork is in my hand and I get to make the decisions. I can feed myself as much Lebanese as I want, and there is plenty to go around. Plenty because our feast is made all the more nourishing by this land that made the feeding possible.

By the time I'm done writing, I realise that Shehadie is right. I do have the opportunity to change a lot, and I'm only invisible if I let myself be.

As I pack the essay into its envelope, ready for posting, I smile, knowing just how far my head and my heart have come.

28

I hate ... therefore I am

Christmas comes and goes in a blur of present-wrapping, food preparation and visits to the endless relatives on our family tree. I realise how much I've changed this year when I sneak out of the house to meet Shehadie for coffee while my parents are visiting some distant relatives in Dural. He spends the whole time laughing at my poor attempts at disguising myself in case we run into anyone I know.

For the first time in a long time, I don't spend New Year's Eve alone, because Dad decides he wants to have a party, and lets me invite Sue and Nicole. Then he spends an hour telling us how much he's broadened his cultural horizons, how lucky we are to be living here, and how the riots and the brawls are a bad chapter that history will do well to forget. I want to roll my eyes, but I don't because I'm proud of him for trying.

Before I know it, the summer holidays are almost over and our family is on holidays at The Entrance, on the Central Coast of New South Wales. On Australia Day, I find myself sitting cross-legged on the sand watching the crowds, enjoying the last days before I return to everyday life.

A lot of Sydney Lebanese come here for their summer holiday, and today they're everywhere, walking around like they own the place. My sisters and I laugh, because we know they're never going to change. Even Andrew comes to sit with us, his rebellious phase seemingly behind him. He's actually been much nicer to be around since he was busted. As he explained to me a few weeks after he was charged, keeping it all a secret had driven him mad, especially with all the pressure and flak he copped from Zayden. All he wanted was justice for his mate, and if that wasn't Aussie camaraderie, what was?

There are people walking about wearing the Aussie flag or green and gold, singing 'Waltzing Matilda' or 'Advance Australia Fair'. Dad joins in, and a man nearby yells, 'Way to go, mate!' Dad laughs even though the tips of his ears turn pink. I seriously want to hide, but I know that if I do, I'll be the hypocrite who hid her head in the sand when she expected everyone else to get their heads out of it and embrace how good they have it here.

My cousins are gathered en masse around a giant beach tent with the word 'Oz' repeated all the way around it, no doubt purchased from Go-Lo and made in China. They're speaking in the loudest Arabic possible, and one of them has *dabke* music blaring from his phone. He has one arm wrapped around his mum while the other makes spirit fingers.

It's the most embarrassing thing in the world, but then an old lady wanders over and starts talking to Mum about where we're from and how nice it is that we're enjoying the national holiday. Mum reciprocates by doing what she does best – force-feeding the lady hummus and tabouli and giving her a few loaves of bread to 'take back to the rest of the group you're with'.

To my horror, she starts teaching the lady how to make hummus, and although she mispronounces nearly everything, the lady looks ecstatic. I wish the *Daily Telegraph* was here to write something positive about the Lebanese, if only to save another seventeen-year-old from an identity crisis like the one I've just been through.

I relocate to the shade under a tree a short distance away from my family, and look around at the vast sea of people on the beach. People of different colours, creeds, styles and personalities. It reminds me of a circular tile I saw outside Parliament House in Canberra that bore the words 'The Commonwealth of Australia'. A man pointed it out to me on a school excursion and said that we weren't just a commonwealth because of Britain but because our commonality was the wealth that each person's background brought to our nation.

I think of the police officer at school who told us, 'To be a wog or a Leb, you have to be an Aussie first.' It's so true – the Lebanese in France or Brazil or Canada wouldn't be caught dead calling themselves Lebs; it's the nickname for Australian Lebanese. And here I've been, fretting about whether or not I belong, when there was a little niche already made for me.

I breathe in the beautiful sea air and flick through my journal in the hope that it will inspire a script or two for the drama subjects I'll be doing as part of my arts degree. Turns out, Dad was thrilled with the idea, if a little concerned about my job prospects post-graduation. Apparently the accounting plan came out of his concern that I was too obliging and go-with-the-flow to determine my own future. I didn't point out to him the irony.

As I read through my journal, I see again all the energy and heartache I've burdened myself with. I've eventually come to understand that my dad's rules, my aunt's rebellion and my mum's subversion aren't always grounded in their ideals. They just have to do what they can with whatever life has dealt them. And I realise something else too: my hate list will never stop growing. I'll always have something to complain about because that's who I am: a sullen, complacent teenager who's working out her strengths, weaknesses, blessings and limitations, and using them to help her leap into the unknown after years of sheltered existence. So I'll let myself keep hating.

I hate that my lack of money means I can't afford to buy a Honda Jazz to zip to and from uni in, and that I'll have to deal with the 1995 Toyota Corolla Dad bought off his friend instead. That's if I manage to pass my driving test next month.

I hate that my favourite jeans are too tight around my mid-thighs and that Thomas was right about me needing to lay off the sweet treats.

I hate that all I ever wanted out of high school was to be acknowledged and remembered, and that I earned this acknowledgement by becoming a feisty snob who called my classmates ignorant after years of putting up with their attitudes because I wanted them to accept me.

I hate the fact that I can be incredibly shallow.

I hate the fact that despite all the headway I've made with my parents, I still have to lie to them if I want to see Shehadie and do normal teenage stuff.

I hate that my first experience of a relationship has to be long-distance.

I hate that I live in a man's world.

I hate the fact that it took me too long to realise that my attitudes were the only baggage worth worrying about.

I hate the fact that I hate so many things.

I hate the fact that I think this is okay, because to me it means acknowledging that life isn't always easy and that I'll have to pinpoint ways to improve it.

I hate that for so long my idea of improving things was crying all alone in my room or whingeing about how no one understood me, when there were wonderful people all around ready to accept me with all my flaws.

I hate the fact that somewhere there'll be another Rita or Vanessa waiting for me to crumble, though I'm determined not to give them that satisfaction.

Hate is such a strong word ... But I LOVE the fact that I'm going to find myself, so that someday I'll stop using it.

ACKNOWLEDGEMENTS

Writing *Hate* has been a long process, so there's a long list of people I am indebted to for their encouragement and support.

A massive thanks to my incredible agent and publishing powerhouse Selwa Anthony, whose knowledge and backing have been instrumental in making this book a reality. A special mention to Kennedy Estephan for the introduction – your generosity will never be forgotten.

Drew Keys, I owe so much of this finished product to your advice and guidance. Thanks especially for that wonderful line: 'To be a wog/Leb you have to be an Aussie first.' It's absolute genius and you deserve the credit for it. I appreciate your help more than you know.

To the incredible team at HarperCollins Australia, who took such great care of me: my publisher, Tegan Morrison, for her unwavering enthusiasm and support, and Cristina Cappelluto, who understood Sophie's dichotomous identity more than I could have hoped for. A big thanks to project editor Chren Byng, publicist Amanda Diaz and Children's campaign manager Tim Miller who pulled everything together.

Thanks also to my editor, Nicola O'Shea, whose comments and edits gave the story just the refinement it was missing.

To the incredibly smart, talented and all-round amazing Rachel Hills for her mentoring from the outset of this writing career; and Tammi Ireland, whose enthusiasm and love have fast made her the friend of a lifetime. There's no measure for how much I appreciate you both.

To the writers who have been sounding boards on everything from industry to writer's block: Megan Burke, Gabrielle Tozer, Bessie Recep, Liv Hambrett, Shitika Anand and Fiona Macdonald. Thanks for the constant inspiration.

And to the cheerleaders who kept me going: Danielle Najem, Regina Assaf, Jamila Ayoub, Gloria Haddad, Hayley Bennett, Viola Doyle and Maha Coorey. And via social media: Abi Moustafa, Allison Tait, Khadija Taiba-Saddik and Scarlett Harris. And of course to Sue Aquilina, who inspired my character Sue, crazy hair included!

Special thanks to Judith Ridge, Steph Little and Liz Goralewski, who offered me advice on the genre.

I'm also thankful for the encouragement from my in-laws: Glenda, Nana, Marilyn, Lizzy, David and Christine; and for cuddles from Jude, Flynn and Lukas, who brought joy to my bad-writing days. And for Mum's family on the other side of the world, who tended to me as though I was royalty when I sat on their veranda writing my final draft, looking out at their old-school Lebanese village.

Thanks to every single person who purchased a copy, or tweeted and Facebooked their excitement at the release. You are making my dream a reality too.

Finally, to my family: my wonderful husband James, for his patience and love. Thank you for always taking such great care of me. My sisters and saving graces, Marie-Claire and Josie, for all the printing and feedback, and Milad and Laura too.

And lastly, to my parents: I hope your children's lives here have made the big trek from the Mother Country worth it. Dad, we have reaped the benefits of your hard work and will always see you as our superhero. I hope I have made you proud. Mum, thanks for your daily prayers, the constant effort you make for your family, and for filling my life with all that is special. Everything that I have ever achieved is a result of your love and sacrifice. This book is yours too. I hope you like it.

ABOUT THE AUTHOR

Sarah Ayoub is a freelance journalist and blogger based in Sydney, Australia. Her work has appeared in various print and online publications, including *Marie-Claire*, *Madison*, *Cosmopolitan*, *House & Garden*, *Sunday Magazine*, *ABC Unleashed*, *Cleo*, *Notebook*, *Shop Til You Drop*, *Frankie*, *Yen*, *Girlfriend* and more. She has taught Journalism at the University of Notre Dame and spoken at numerous industry events with the Emerging Writers' Festival, NSW Writers' Centre, the Walkley Foundation, Vibewire and more.

To find out more about Sarah, you can follow her on Facebook and Twitter or check out her blog at http://sarahayoub.com.